AN URCHIN OF MEANS

APRIL WHITE

Seattle7Writers.org

CORAZON
ENTERTAINMENT

The Baker Street Series

An Urchin of Means
A Lady in Waiting (coming soon)
A Pocket of Hope (coming soon)

The Immortal Descendants Series

Marking Time
Tempting Fate
Changing Nature
Waging War
Cheating Death

An Urchin of Means. Copyright 2018 by April White
All rights reserved. Published by Corazon Entertainment
Palos Verdes Peninsula, CA

Edited by Angela Houle
Cover Design by Penny Reid

ISBN 978-1-946161-13-0
Library of Congress Control Number: 2017919428

First American edition, January, 2018

"Yes: I am a dreamer.

For a dreamer is one who can only find his way by moonlight, and his punishment is that he sees the dawn before the rest of the world."

Oscar Wilde

TABLE OF CONTENTS

Author's Note

The books of the Baker Street Series stand alone. They are the adventures and mysteries of Ringo Devereux in Victorian London as he keeps company with the likes of Arthur Conan Doyle and Oscar Wilde. The story of Ringo's origins as a time-traveling Victorian urchin and thief can be found in The Immortal Descendants series. Book one of that series, *Marking Time*, is free and all five books are available at all e-book retailers.

CHAPTER 1 – THIEF

The little guttersnipe was fast, I'd give it that.

Quick-fingered and fleet-footed, for all it was ten years old, and there I'd been, cutting across Regent's Park with my arms full of books as if I were the most oblivious nob in London. Damn, but I was in no mood to run. The entire month of August had been hot, and the camouflage I wore – the well-cut coat and fussy cravat of a respectable university student – was stifling. But if I didn't tuck the books away somewhere and sprint after it, I'd lose Charlie's money, and I certainly did not want to tell my wife the advance for her illustrations had been lifted from my pocket by a street rat.

The thief clearly hadn't expected me to give chase. It was of indeterminate gender, small, slender, barefoot, and wearing its own camouflage of street grime. Grime was different than filth –

1

grime coated the skin and clothes with good, clean dirt but didn't smell of sewers or sweat. Filth stank and made people wary, therefore proper pickpockets tended to be fairly fastidious in their grooming habits under the dirt.

My annoyance grew in direct proportion to the distance we covered, and despite my longer legs, this rat had remarkable stamina. It took a turn out of the land of the quite-well-off, and darted into the dangerous territory of the very well-to-do, where the degrees of wealth ran from having one country manor to having ten. I hadn't called out for help yet – my own habit toward invisibility being too ingrained – but when the street rat sprinted toward the Langham Hotel, I finally knew how to trap it.

"Stop! Thief!"

My voice had a pleasing boom and caused people to look around for the big man they assumed must go with it. I was not overly tall – early years of hunger had likely stunted what may have been a large frame if I'd had proper feeding – but my voice had become surprisingly deep. It was menacing when I needed it to be, and authoritative enough to let me blend into the wealthy clientele of the Langham.

A slightly startled doorman, sporting the name John Hartwell on his uniform, acted without thought and grabbed my thief as she – yes, upon closer examination of delicate collar bones and elfin features, the street rat appeared to be female – attempted to slip into the hotel. I had perhaps ten seconds before Hartwell thought better of holding such a wriggly little thing and let her go; ten seconds in which to proclaim my authority over the glaring creature and retrieve Charlie's money. The shreds of my own dignity, as a pickpocket's victim, would be less simple to recover.

"Right. I'll just have my wallet back then," I said to the creature as I approached.

"I ain't got nothin' of yers," she snarled back, squirming violently in the doorman's hands.

I ignored her and met Hartwell's startled eyes. He was surprised, perhaps, that I was young and lean and didn't fit the voice I'd used to command the rat's capture. "I'll take this little vermin off your hands and remove it from your very fine establishment, if you please?" I slid into a posh, upper-crust accent – I'd been practicing such mimicry for months, and it had become frighteningly second-nature. As such things still did in the English class system, the cadence of expensive English boarding school had the desired effect. It baffled me that such a simple thing as an accent could induce a person to compliance, and yet the evidence was right in front of me.

"Right-o, Guv." Hartwell shoved the pickpocket forward, and she stumbled into my hands. She tried to wrench herself away before I could get a solid grip on her bony shoulders, but I had her spun around, one arm twisted up behind her back, before she could so much as spit, which I expected would have come next if I had been so foolish as to face her.

3

"All right, Rat. Out you go," I murmured into her ear as I marched her through the door and back out to the street.

"I'm no rat," she protested sharply as she attempted to bite the arm I'd wrapped across her shoulders.

"If it scurries like a rat, and squeaks like a rat, it must be a rat. The question is whether you'll escape this particular trap intact. That was my wife's money you stole, and I'll have it back now."

The girl scoffed. "'Whoever 'eard of a wife with 'er own bob? It all belongs to ye, don't it?"

"It is money she *earned*. Perhaps even you can appreciate the significance of that." I had my coin purse from the band at her waist and tucked into my trouser pocket before she felt the slightest motion. Despite having been ridiculously careless enough to get pickpocketed in the first place, my own dexterity, which had fed me for much of my early life, remained firmly habitual.

"'Ere now! That's mine ye be takin'!" Her voice screeched alarmingly, and for one quick moment I feared she would draw heroic eyes to her plight. Doormen I could reason with, but men or women of the social justice warrior class were more than I had patience for in the London heat with a wriggling pickpocket in my hands.

I leaned close to her ear and dropped my voice to a menacing snarl, adopting the most effective accent for the job. "Ye'll 'ear this once, and only once. Marylebone is mine. From Regent's Park to Mayfair and Fitzrovia, the only nimble-fingered guttersnipes

4

that work 'ere work fer me. And since ye don't work fer me, *ye don't work 'ere.*"

The girl had frozen for exactly one second at the knife's edge in my voice, then gave up her struggle as a bad job. She wasn't afraid of me, but perhaps my accent had convinced her I wasn't quite the nob she'd first believed. My awareness of the street around us had grown more pronounced as I spoke – the sounds of horses' hooves told me the carriage that had pulled up behind me was driven by four spry Morgans, one of which was going lame. Conversations around us quickly catalogued themselves in my brain as important, like the young man gossiping with another about a scandalous baccarat game attended by the prince, or trivial, like the wife accusing her husband of appreciating another woman. And ringing above it all was the jangle of coins in a man's pocket that included the dull ring of a solid gold sovereign. I knew the rat had heard all these things as well, and I wondered if perhaps I should make a point of behaving like a tough for a few minutes each day to stay sharp.

The lunch crowd was beginning to thicken the street with the posh and powerful who regularly dined at places such as the Langham. I pulled the girl away from the hotel entrance toward Portland Place. We turned the corner to avoid a couple approaching the steps and nearly collided with a tall man in a frock coat who walked with the long stride of the very confident.

"Ringo, my dear young man! How lovely to see you!" The man's deep, cultured voice was instantly recognizable, though it had the unfortunate effect of jolting my concentration. The rat jerked her arm free, and I succeeded in catching only a bit of the collar of her shirt, which neatly disintegrated with age.

I looked up to find the enormously amused Oscar Wilde smiling down at me. "Oh dear, I do hope I didn't frighten that poor child away from whatever nefarious task you had planned for the creature," he said cheerfully.

"*She* had just successfully picked my pocket. I was merely attempting to restore a shred of my professional dignity while relieving her of the ill-gotten gain," I said as I straightened the infernal cravat.

"Your professional dignity?" Wilde ventured.

I spoke the truth with just enough humor in my tone as to render it unbelievable. "Evidently, my previous life as a thief and pickpocket didn't leave identifying marks."

Wilde's booming laughter at my apparent joke carried to the front doors of the Langham, in the direction of which he was suddenly propelling me. "Come to lunch with me. I'm meeting two other gentlemen of the storytelling persuasion, and they will wish to hear the tale of your adventure as much as I."

I thought of my books, hidden behind a bench in Regent's Park, and I thought of the long walk in the blazing midday sun to retrieve them before my planned expedition to study at the

6

University College library, where I'd spent the past year being a respectable student of philosophy and physics, with enough history, science, and letters to keep things entertaining.

I held my hand out to shake, and it was instantly enveloped in his ridiculously large, yet remarkably gentle grip. "I'm delighted to see you again, Mr. Wilde. I was on my way to study physics, but I believe the restoration of my dignity might require a thoroughly self-effacing recounting of the day's events. Thank you for the invitation."

He clapped me on the shoulder. "Good man! Education is an admirable thing, but it is well to remember from time to time that nothing that is worth knowing can be taught. And if it assuages your conscience, I am certain there was an element of physics at play in the encounter with your thief."

I chuckled as I recalled an image of the street rat dropping off a wall, tumbling down an embankment, and leaping a leashed bulldog that turned and snapped at her heels. She was resourceful and intrepid – qualities I rarely had the occasion to admire among my recent acquaintances.

"Indeed, there was." I looked back over my shoulder for the young thief I knew was long gone, and then allowed myself to be directed back into the elegant foyer of the Langham Hotel.

Chapter 2 – The Langham Lunch

The remarkable thing about the Langham lunch was that I'd read about it in the library at Elian Manor, the country house of very dear friends who didn't actually live in this century. I did not realize the significance of the date or the location when Wilde introduced me to the first gentleman, a Mr. Joseph Stoddart from America. But the next gentleman's name was known to me, and I made an instant connection to the history book I'd read in my previous life, or if one insisted on a literal interpretation of time – that I *would* read in more than a hundred years. I shook the man's hand with equal amounts of interest and alarm.

"Mr. Conan Doyle. It is a pleasure to meet you, sir." I attempted to keep the awe down to a mild case of wonder at finding myself in the company of the famed playwright, Wilde, the publisher of Lippincott's magazine, Stoddart, and the author of the mysteries of Sherlock Holmes, Arthur Conan Doyle, but I was sure I failed quite dismally. For his part, Wilde seemed privately amused at my discomfiture.

"Tell us, Mr. Devereux, about your encounter with this feculent bit of London underworld," Wilde said, with a particular emphasis on the surname, because he knew it had not always been mine. We'd been seated at a table in a quiet corner of the restaurant, and a carefully expressionless waiter came to the table.

After we placed our orders, I smiled ruefully at my companions. "It is, sadly, a brief and miserable tale of a young man who knows much better than to walk with an armful of books, thereby leaving his pockets free to be explored by the first stealthy fingers he attracts."

"But why does an armful of books matter?" asked Stoddart. Had I been a betting man, I would have laid thousands that he'd be the target of every pickpocket and thief in London.

"When one's arms are occupied by heavy things, one is often more worried about keeping the load balanced than by what may be happening in one's pockets. This thief was far more light-footed than most. Not a surprise, really, this being the end of the summer after all. She sleeps close by however, so I feel certain I'll see her again."

"What does the end of summer have to do with the price of tea in China, and how on earth do you know where she sleeps?" Conan Doyle laughed incredulously.

9

I shrugged. "The vast majority of child thieves in this city are poor. The workhouses give out shoes just as winter sets in, but children are still growing. By the spring, they've outgrown whatever shreds of footwear they have left. Very few barefoot pickpockets can sneak up on a person at the beginning of summer, when their feet are still soft and the sharp stones make an uneven gait audible to any man. But by the end of summer their callouses are firmly in place, and a quiet, even footfall can go unnoticed by all but the most careful listeners."

Conan Doyle and Stoddart stared at me, while Wilde's expression was practically gleeful.

"I had no idea!" Conan Doyle exclaimed, unsurprisingly. Most people didn't think about a destitute child's feet during the winter, and if they did, it was generally only to shake their head and cluck at the dirty bare feet.

"And where this thief lives? How did you determine that?" Wilde asked.

"It is a hot day, as you will have noticed. The St. Marylebone Workhouse is close enough to Regent's Park, where I was accosted, that it is conceivable for the child to live, or at least eat there. They have a new women's wing, apparently with a bathing room and hot running water. This girl had bathed recently enough that she'd collected no rank odors in her wanderings, and her shirt was threadbare from frequent washings rather than mere age. It was also unfashionable enough, and of sufficient quality, to indicate that it had been donated, as those whose wealth comes with a dash of guilty conscience do to workhouses, rather than stolen from a wash line. Furthermore, had she traveled much farther to Regent's, she would have carried the scent of her neighborhood with her – the poorest ones always have the distinctive scents of cooking, smoke, and sewage – and would not have been so fresh as to have been able to sprint all the way here before I caught up to her."

Stoddart wrinkled his nose. "St. Marylebone Workhouse has a stench that is unmistakable."

"That is because you are staying in Pimlico, sir. The neighborhood where one resides becomes invisible to the senses after a time, one more reason I assume she stays in Marylebone, which is where I reside. Unfamiliar neighborhoods are like new perfumes and must be gotten used to."

Conan Doyle leaned forward in disbelief. "My good man, you cannot possibly know that Stoddart is staying in Pimlico. I, myself, found the lodging for him just days ago, and he was ill in bed until only yesterday."

"The Grosvenor Pub has an excellent chicken soup, does it not, Mr. Stoddart? I assume that's where you went once you were able to keep the food down."

Stoddart gripped the table, and he made to rise from his seat. "Have you been following me, sir?" he demanded.

"Sit down, Joseph," Wilde said mildly.

"Explain yourself, Mr. Devereux." Stoddart was fuming. I forgave him his pique as the product of fear, and I attempted to dispel the mystery so as to relieve him of it.

"It's very simple, Mr. Stoddart. Peeking out of the inside pocket of your jacket is your horse tram ticket. Between that and the small smudge of horse dung on your shoe, it was clearly your mode of transportation to this meeting. That you used public transportation would indicate a rental room rather than a man staying with friends. As to location, the horse trams are run primarily along a north-south route through London, a route that includes Vauxhall and Pimlico. There are several guesthouses with rooms to let near the wharves at Pimlico, and because those wharves are the landing place for much of the shipping traffic from America, and because you'd been ill for much of your time aboard your ship, it seems logical to assume that you had taken rooms near the wharf. I happen to know Grosvenor Pub and have enjoyed the chicken soup there on several occasions when I've been unwell. The small stain of broth on your sleeve would indicate that you, too, had dined recently on soup. The Grosvenor is just across from the wharf at Pimlico, ergo my assumption that you had likely eaten there."

Stoddart's anger seemed to have slipped out of the room with its tail between its legs, and his next question held a note of wonder. "And the fact that you believe I've been ill?"

I looked at him in all seriousness. "Mr. Stoddart, trust me when I say you appear to be on the mend. However, your suit, well-cut and fashionable though it is, hangs loosely on you, and the lines of your cheekbones look as though they were carved in stone. You have neither slept well nor seen the sun, which, having arrived as you did after an Atlantic crossing during high summer, leads me to surmise you spent much of the time below decks decidedly *not* sleeping. Your recent meal at the Grosvenor gave you a bit of energy – enough to make it to this luncheon – but in my humble opinion, you could do with a few more days of rest before you venture out to explore London."

"And when I do, I believe I'd like to hire you as my guide," Stoddart's tone was laced with mild respect.

"I'd be happy to show you our city, sir. Just as soon as you're up to it," I said politely.

"I should like to join you on a tour led by Mr. Devereux," said Conan Doyle. "Somehow I think it would be very different than one we might get from even the most seasoned hackney driver."

I shrugged. "One must know the right drivers."

Wilde burst out in booming laughter that drew the gaze of most of the social elite dining at the Langham Hotel that day. "Ringo, you have no idea how delighted I am to have run into you today. This is the sort of conversation that belongs on the stage, or perhaps in a story. Gentlemen, I do believe I might steal bits of

13

our luncheon, and pieces of your souls, to immortalize in words. Would you mind very much?"

Conan Doyle was still staring at me, as he'd been through most of our meal. "Ringo? That's your given name."

"It is the name I am called, yes."

"An odd name. I'm very fond of odd names, especially in my mystery stories."

I almost said that I knew, but fortunately swallowed the words before they could complicate things even further. Wilde arched an eyebrow at me in a way that suggested he'd like to have heard the words I didn't utter, but I gave him a politely charming smile and changed the subject.

After our excellent meal, during which much of the conversation revolved around the writings of both Wilde and Conan Doyle, I reluctantly rose from the table. "Gentlemen, it has been a pleasure to have met and dined with you. It is time for me to retrieve my books from their hiding spot in Regent's Park and go home."

The other men stood and we shook hands all around, then Wilde walked with me part of the way toward the door. "I believe there are many more stories you could tell, my dear man. Perhaps you and your lady wife would allow me to call one day to hear them?"

"You know I am married?" I had met Oscar Wilde only once, in circumstances very different from the ones in which I now found myself.

"I do now," he said mischievously. "You have the look of a man well cared for, and though I may wish differently, it is clearly a young woman who has lovingly trimmed your hair and chosen that very colorful cravat to liven up such a boringly fashionable coat." He shook my hand with genuine warmth. "I should like to meet your Mrs. Devereux, and to hear the story of this name you did not carry when last we met."

Chapter 3 – Baker Street

My books were gone from behind the bench in Regent's Park, but the small, dusty footprint I found on a stone a few steps away gave me a fair indication of who had taken them. I thought it unlikely that the street rat could read, so I assumed they'd been long-since sold to cover what I was sure she believed I owed her for removing Charlie's coin purse from her possession.

I arrived home in a slightly annoyed, mostly resigned state of mind, still much too warm to be wearing all the gear a proper Englishman of this time had to wear in order to blend into the scenery. My biggest problem was that I didn't believe I was a proper Englishman, and therefore, everything chafed – the tight coats, tight trousers, silk cravats, top hats, stiff leather shoes, social status, etiquette, accents, expectations, and most profoundly, rules.

I slipped in through the mews to the back of the house that had been built at number 14 Cornwall Terrace. It was on land that my mother-in-law, Valerie Grayson, had been gifted by Queen Mary Tudor. It was Crown land, originally part of the Upper Baker Street tract, the boundaries of which had been moved in 1811 when the Prince Regent commissioned architect John Nash to produce a master plan for the area.

For one who didn't know Charlie's and my history, the dates of various events in our lives would seem impossible. I'd been born in approximately 1870, though I wasn't exactly sure of either the date or the year, and Charlie was about a year younger than I. She, however, had been adopted by Valerie, who was from the sixteenth century, and spent several months in 1554 while my own adventures included travel from the fifteenth to the twenty-first centuries with our friend Saira. Although we'd each found dear friends in other times, when we married, Charlie and I decided to return "home" to our own time. The complexity of our background meant I was not quite so excited at the prospect of a visit from Oscar Wilde. He was far too intelligent a man to be satisfied with the usual explanation that Charlie had been left the house by a wealthy grandmother who had lived and died far removed from London. Although Wilde had his own gifts that would allow him to understand the basics of our time traveling past, they just weren't stories that I shared. Consequences of such stories had the potential to result in a nice little visit to Bedlam, or, for the particularly unlucky, a complete split in time. I'd seen one once and it wasn't pretty.

17

Charlie found me in the bedroom as I was changing into my preferred around-the-house-wear of denim jeans and a soft cotton t-shirt. The housekeeper, Mrs. Mac, was the only other person who had ever seen the twenty-first-century clothes I'd been loath to part with, and she already thought we were mad not to employ a whole household staff to cook and clean and wait on us as though we were useless lumps of flesh with no survival skills of our own. One strange outfit more or less wasn't going to change her opinion of our relative sanity.

My wife came up behind me, not trying to be stealthy in the slightest. "There's a big pot of Cullen skink bubbling away on the stove if you're hungry. Mrs. Mac bought five pounds of smoked haddock from the fishmonger because she said his wife is with child again." Charlie slipped her arms around my waist. "Hmm, but you smell of lobster bisque and fresh bread."

I turned around to hold her. She came up just under my chin, and her hair smelled like lilacs. Having her in my arms was the only thing that allowed the day to seep from me – this day, any day – none of them mattered when I held my wife.

"I had lunch with Oscar Wilde," I murmured into her hair.

She pulled back to stare at me. Everything about Charlie's face was delicate and perfectly in proportion to her tiny loveliness – except her eyes. They were strong and knowing and held more life than most people ever lived. They were so blue they were almost purple, and her surprise showed in them with nearly audible questions. "Tell me," she said as she drew me to the window seat and curled up on the bench across from me. It was our favorite place to sit and watch small children run in the park while their governesses gossiped on the benches.

I held her hands in mine and played with my ring on her finger while I told her the details of my day. She listened patiently, asking questions about the girl's appearance and details of where we'd run. She stifled giggles when I recounted the conversation at lunch, and looked thoughtful at the notion that Wilde would call on us. And when I was finally silent, she let the air settle quietly around us for a long moment before she spoke.

"You should tell him," she said finally.

She meant Wilde.

"I suppose I could. He's a Seer, or at least comes from a Seer family. I'm not sure how skilled he is, but I'm fairly certain he understands about Time and time travel," I said. My first meeting with Oscar Wilde had been accidental and felt like a lifetime ago. I had taken my friends Saira, the time traveler, and Tom, who also had a bit of that skill, to St. Etheldreda's Church to listen to whatever writer or artist was speaking. Neither of them was native to the Victorian Era, and Saira had been the first to recognize Wilde's words because she had studied them in school. We had left that church just before dawn after a long night spent in conversation with the writer and the priest, richer in wisdom and friendship than when we'd arrived.

For Oscar Wilde, barely a year had passed since that night. For Charlie and me, the world and all its rules as we knew them had completely changed.

Charlie stroked one hand down my arm to return my attention to her. "You have no friends here, Ringo." Her voice was quiet, but the words struck my solar plexus quite uncomfortably.

"I have you; friend, lover, wife. It's more than I could ever have imagined."

"But you deserve a bigger life than this. We keep to this house and the university, we have far more means than we need or necessarily know what to do with, and we have only ourselves to inspire us to something more."

She wasn't wrong, though it felt a bit like failure to admit it out loud. "It does feel rather centripetal in here."

Charlie tilted her head in a way that reminded me of a clever sparrow. "It's Latin, but what does it mean?"

"Centri – the center, petere – to seek. You, my lovely wife, are the center of the universe to which I will always naturally gravitate. What I have failed to do is find those things *from which* to gravitate toward you. I imagine I've become dreadfully boring."

Charlie's laughter sounded as though a merry band of fairies had just danced through the room, and I would readily admit that my heart beat faster in response.

"You could never be boring. When *they*, whoever they usually are, wrote the definition of boring, they took one look at you and said *boring is decidedly not that man.* You do, however, need someone more than me to talk to so that we remember never to take each other for granted."

"Talking to others is risky for people with such secrets about the past, and even more dangerously, the future, as we have," I said with more seriousness in my voice than I intended.

"Secrets become exhausting when there is no one with whom to lighten their load." Charlie seemed sad when she said it, and I sensed her sadness was for me.

"I have no secrets from you. For now, it is enough," I said as I cupped her cheek in my hand.

Something moved in my peripheral vision, and I looked out the window down to the park below. The late afternoon shadows were long, and the small children had all gone inside for early suppers before bedtime. A rabbit darted from a small copse of trees and across the wide lawn. Something had sent the rabbit running from that copse.

The short hair at the back of my neck prickled with the instinct of one who used to *be* the watcher. Someone was out there, watching … us.

We hadn't yet lit any candles, and I slid off the window seat and gestured for Charlie to back out of sight. She did so immediately, and I appreciated the trust she had in me.

"I feel watched," I murmured to her as though whoever was outside could also hear me.

Charlie stood at the side of the window and looked around the park landscape as far as she could see. "It's very still out there – no dogs or children to have gotten your attention."

"I'm going out while it's still light," I said.

She looked me up and down. "Not like that, you're not. Not unless you want to be arrested for vagrancy and locked up at St. Marylebone's."

I sighed and quickly stripped out of my beloved twenty-first-century clothes. They were becoming a bit threadbare with washings, but the denim was the approximate texture of silk. I would give them up when they fell apart, but not a minute sooner.

"My thief is probably getting meals at St. Marylebone's," I said as I tugged on my proper British trousers and tucked in the long tails of my proper British shirt.

"Then I will go tomorrow and see what they need. Shoes for the children, you said?"

I kissed Charlie quickly, both hands holding her face. "Thank you for finding me in this world. I didn't know how very much I needed you."

She smiled and hugged me tightly, and something in my expression made her laugh. "You look just like a little boy coming down the stairs in anticipation of presents under the tree," she continued.

22

"I wouldn't know what that's like; I didn't have Christmas when I was a little boy. Maybe I'll get to see it on another small face someday." We were in the upper hall, and I leapt over the bannister to hit the landing halfway down, then slid the rest of the way on the handrail. I did this at least once a week to contribute to my share of the housework. Clean bannisters for a happy home, and all that.

I used the mews as my entrance and exit to our house almost exclusively. I doubted any of our neighbors would know me for the man of the house if they saw me in my own study. My ingrained instincts for camouflage preferred the relative anonymity, and so far I hadn't needed the protection of status. I hoped to keep it that way.

I wasn't fastidious by nature, but I had a habit of keeping hinges and locks oiled and in good repair. Our doors actually had modern locks hidden behind the skeleton key openings, and we had become very good at masking the appropriate key as we used it so as not to raise suspicion at its strange appearance. Modern lock picks like I had could do the job on the tumblers, but nineteenth-century ones had no chance. So far, no one had put them to the test, for which I was grateful.

The heat was still stifling, despite the sun's recent departure beneath the horizon. It was a time of evening I loved because the light was at its most interesting. This evening, however, the shadows were fickle in their loyalty, and I crept along the side of the house aware that whatever hid me could easily hide another.

It was nearly nine o'clock, and the street was deserted. We didn't tend to get a lot of drunks or vagrants wandering Regent's Park at night – it was too far removed from London proper and too close to a very large workhouse with hot meals and hundreds of beds. Any movement in the park would either be animal or suspect, which was the primary reason I was dressed like a gentleman, despite the damnable whiteness of the shirt.

There was a copse of trees across from the ones in which I'd seen movement, and I slid around the outside of the walled garden to blend into the sturdy trunks as well as one might in the circumstances. It had been easier to blend when I'd been a practicing urchin, with dirt and general grime providing much better cover than starched white shirts ever would.

Some instinct made me look up into the tree above me, and I was startled to see a grimy little elfin face staring down at me from a height of about fifteen feet.

"Right. You." I grumbled the words even as the sight of my thief actually filled me with relief.

She squeaked as I started to climb, and leapt to a branch on the nearest tree. I expected the move, and swung over to a lower branch on the same tree to continue my climb. The little rat didn't like that one bit, and her next jump was almost to the edge of her ability. I bit back a concerned noise as she just barely caught the branch, and I let her get down to the ground before I jumped down to follow.

She took off into the park, which is what I'd hoped she would do. There were no patrols in Regent's Park until well after midnight, so for my purposes, it was as close to a playground as I'd ever had. In my restlessness since Charlie and I had chosen to come back to London in this time, I had gone for nightly runs through the park at whatever speed made my heart pump fastest.

The thief darted across the river on the footpath near the receiving house, then cut through the trees toward the South Villa. I would likely have stayed to the left, where the trees were thickest, until I'd gotten to the Inner Circle road, but she was heading toward the open grounds of the South Villa, and I wondered what she had planned.

Ah, there it was – the wall. She scampered up and over the top of it, clearly anticipating that I wouldn't follow. When I did, the shock on her face was visible even in the twilight, and she picked up speed and swerved around the handsome building that once housed George Bishop's observatory in a dome on the roof.

The girl sprinted across the road and hurdled another wall. I followed right behind, mentally mapping the Royal Botanic Society's gardens for places in which to trap my little rat. The meteorological instruments section would do nicely if I could manage to drive her that way, though at the moment she seemed inclined to veer toward the palmery.

It felt good to run with a purpose, unlike earlier in the day when I'd done so with grim determination. I would even admit to having added some unnecessary flips over barriers and down from walls. The rat's own determination blinded her to my showing off, but I was having too much fun to care.

The girl was small and fierce, with a deep wariness that reminded me a bit of Charlie when I'd first met her. My wife was the younger sister of Jack the Ripper's last victim, and had seen the worst of London's underworld even before she'd witnessed her sister's murder. Perhaps it was the fate of all frightened, underfed children that they vaguely resembled the magic creatures of the woods as this one certainly did, with black, short-cropped hair, the brown skin of a sailor's get, and enormous eyes that had seen too much to ever look innocent.

Doubtless it was what I'd once looked like too, until good food and access to twenty-first century medicine in the last few years had allowed me to grow bigger than the poor sods with rotten teeth at twenty and tuberculosis by twenty-five.

I swung a little wider than I strictly needed to, and it had the desired effect of nudging the girl to the right, toward the part of the garden where the wall was smoother and hedges were thicker. She was getting tired, too – a function of not enough food that day, I'd guess.

"We're having Cullen skink tonight if you'd like some!" I shouted, for no other reason than I was suddenly famished myself.

The thief stopped so suddenly, I swerved so as not to run her over. She put both hands on her hips and glared at me with the ferocity of a Pict warrior. "Wot the bleedin' 'ell is Cullen skink?"

It was a struggle to keep a straight face.

"A potato and onion soup made from smoked haddock. Our housekeeper's Scottish, and she thinks we don't eat enough," I said.

The girl scoffed. "Ye're a right barber's cat, ye are."

I shrugged. "Makes no difference to me if you come, but you're invited."

I turned and started back toward my house. I knew I had her attention by the arms that crossed her front, though. She might have been trying to look tough, but from where I stood, it looked as though she held her belly tight to keep it from rumbling.

She moved like a cat behind me, and I ignored her. I made a point to scramble up walls and flip off them, just because I knew I had an audience this time. It wasn't until we reached the footbridge that she finally spoke again.

"Why?"

I had to run back through my words to realize she was responding to the invitation. I shrugged again and kept my tone utterly casual. "I got hungry. Figured you might be too. And Mrs. Mac made enough to feed an army, as she always does."

"It's a trap," she said glumly.

"Don't steal anything else from me and you're free to go." I opened the side gate to the garden and pocketed the key.

"I could climb the wall, ye know."

"Sure, but then my beasts might eat you," I said as two mutts of indeterminate parentage came bounding out of the house to greet me. Gryf and Huff were street dogs Charlie had fed until they came inside the garden, and now they wouldn't leave its walls unless we were with them. "Gryf! Huff! Heel!" I commanded, using the voice to its full potential. The dogs came right to heel, and I wondered if Charlie had been training them with extra treats. "Good beasts," I said, ruffling their ears.

"What kind of names are those?" the girl asked in the voice I was coming to realize meant she was forcing herself into belligerence so she didn't bolt.

"They're the names of magical places, Gryffindor and Hufflepuff," said Charlie from the servants' entrance.

The girl nearly did bolt then, but she must have seen my face light up like a candle, which it always did when I saw my wife. "Hello, my love. We have a guest for dinner."

CHAPTER 4 – JESS

"I saw you coming across the park. The table in the kitchen's all set," Charlie said with a smile at the thief.

Gryf and Huff led the way into the house as if they were a pack of dogs rather than just two, swirling their people into the room. The kitchen was my favorite room in our house – in any house, really, unless there was a library, and then it was a tie. Our libraries were a work in progress, which meant we'd only been able to fill the shelves of one room, and the shelves I'd had built in the gaming room were only half-full. I'd tried to turn the ballroom into the library, but Charlie wisely pointed out it would be too expensive to heat in the winter. The formal dining room was next on the list. We only used it on the rare occasions when Valerie visited us. Valerie had died in the late sixteenth century and left us the house. She could also travel through time, though she only used it to visit us on special occasions, so as not to impose herself on her son-in-law, I supposed.

I grinned to myself as I imagined trying to explain that circumstance to the average Victorian without causing cranial detonation.

Charlie directed the girl to a seat next to her place at the big kitchen table. I washed my hands at the kitchen sink, dried them on the dogs' heads just because there's such a thing as too clean, then carried the heavy pot of soup off the stove. Charlie put a trivet on the table and laid a fresh loaf of crusty French bread onto a board. She handed me the bread knife while she got a pot of newly-churned butter. "Don't crush the bread when you slice it – it's hot," she warned me.

The girl stared, her big eyes practically bugging out of her elfin face at our movements around the kitchen.

"Ye're sittin' *'ere*?" She finally asked, clearly dumbfounded. "Are ye the servants then?"

Charlie chuckled quietly. "It's our house, and we sit where we like. You're welcome to go sit in the formal dining room if you'd prefer, but you'd better take a candelabra if you do. The shadows in there move in the most awful ways when one is alone."

I sat at my place across from them as Charlie ladled soup into all of our bowls, and I tried very hard not to massacre the bread.

I obviously failed, because the girl rolled her eyes and took the knife from me in a way that shouted that she thought I was an idiot. She then flipped the bread over and proceeded to cut delicately through the hot crust as though it were butter. Charlie smirked at me and then placed the girl's soup in front of her. "You're hired." The thief almost cut her own finger when her head jerked up to see Charlie smiling at her. "If you want a job, you're hired," my wife repeated.

"To cut bread, ma'am?" For the first time in my short acquaintance with her, the girl sounded her age, which was ten if it was a day.

"First, I'm too young to be ma'am. Second, yes, I'd like you to cut whatever bread I make until your skill shames my husband into doing it properly. But if you're willing, I'd like to hire you for other things too. Our housekeeper, Mrs. Mac, is as strong as an ox, but she's neither quick nor agile, and if I send her on an errand, I don't see her for hours. I'm sure Ringo could use your help as well, cataloguing books in the libraries and keeping the various folders in his study from becoming a flesh-eating monster we one day find him buried beneath."

"I don't read, ma'am."

Charlie shrugged. "Neither did I. Ringo taught me."

I'd been quietly dipping bread into the soup and eating with my hands while I watched the thief absorb the words Charlie had spoken.

"What's your name?" I finally asked.

The wonder that had been growing in her eyes was instantly replaced by wariness. I held my hand across the table to her and she flinched back. "Mine's Ringo Devereux, and this is Charlie, my wife."

Her tiny hand hesitated a long moment as she stared at mine. I guessed she was looking at the many scars and tiny cuts a person gets when they spend their childhood climbing buildings to break into upper story windows. Finally, she took my proffered hand and shook it. "I'm called Jess."

"Jess," my wife said, putting her own hand out to shake. "It's nice to meet you."

Charlie and I returned our attention to our soup for a few bites to give Jess the next move if she wanted it. It seemed she did.

"Ye're both from the street, but ye don't talk like it."

That was interesting. I swallowed the bit of bread I'd been chewing and met Jess's gaze. There was appreciation there rather than suspicion.

"Why do you think we're from the street?" A successful pickpocket had to develop great observational skills in order to eat and stay free. I was intrigued to see whether this one had them.

Jess seemed to know I was testing her because she looked straight into my eyes as she answered. "Yer 'ands, first of all. To get that many scars and not be thick, beefy sausages, ye're not a laborer – not that ye 'ave the size for it, for all ye 'ave the bellow

32

of one. And ye're too fast to 'ave learned to run at school. Ye learned it on the street, same as me. Also, I 'eard a bit of Whitechapel in yer words when ye tried to threaten me. Nice bit o' fluff that one. Most wouldn't fancy meetin' that voice in a dark alley, would they?"

Charlie smirked. She'd laughed earlier when I had told her about using the menace, which is what she called my toughest tone of voice, on Jess outside the Langham.

"Also, ye're right uncomfortable in the fancy togs. Ye weren't born to 'em."

My wife's smirk became a giggle, and I couldn't help the answering smile when I looked at her. We had known each other for months before I'd ever heard her laugh, and each giggle or chuckle was still more precious to me than all the coins in the world.

I returned my gaze to Jess. "What about Charlie? Why do you think she's from the street?"

Jess shrugged and looked at her soup. "Who else would 'ave ye?"

Charlie's burst of laughter was crystalline, and I breathed it in. Jess looked shyly at my wife, and I could tell the sound of her laugh affected the girl as well.

"So, will you take the job, Jess?" Charlie asked her.

The girl stood suddenly. "I'd best get goin' before my bed's gone."

33

"At St. Marylebone's?" I asked.

Jess glared at me. "Did ye 'ave me followed then?"

I shrugged and made my tone casual. This one was like a stray cat who'd been kicked one too many times. "You're too clean under all that dirt to be a proper street rat. Your clothes have been washed, and you get one meal a day, but not two. You're not covered in rat bites, so you don't sleep under bridges, nor do you scratch, so you've been deloused. You knew where to find me, which means you'd followed me from here, and the edges of Regent's Park are not obvious buzzer hunting grounds, so that tells me you came for the scenery and then found an easy mark."

I scoffed at myself and looked at Charlie. "I need to make myself a canvas or leather backpack — something that won't look too out of place. A satchel strap is too easy to cut, and arms full of books just invite thieves." I kept my tone conversational on purpose. The books were gone, even as the girl who likely stole them stood at our table, watching us warily.

Charlie looked up at her, an equally casual expression on her face. She knew how not to spook a child with accusations when kindness might be more effective. "We can find a bed for you here if you like."

The girl shook her head quickly. "I share my bed. If I'm not back to lay my 'ead on the pillow, someone'll take what's mine." She grabbed what was left of her piece of bread and then dipped her head. "Thank ye for the supper."

34

She strode to the door and slipped out before the dogs could even get up to escort her. Gryf did manage to raise his head to watch her go, but Huff was out cold at my feet.

Charlie and I watched the closed door for a long moment, perhaps hoping it would be opened by a girl with second thoughts, or perhaps merely remembering a time when we had been that young, that frightened, and that lonely. My wife reached for my hand and squeezed it gently.

"She'll be back," we said at the same time.

CHAPTER 5 – THE BAKERY

Charlie was still sleeping, and Gryf had taken my spot on the bed. Huff walked at my side through the park as he did every morning on our way to the baker for fresh rolls. The morning air had the crisp freshness that signaled a shift in the weather – a welcome change from the heat that had gripped London in its sweaty fist and wrung all the good humor from its inhabitants.

The baker, who was inexplicably named Mr. Milliner, was deep in conversation with his wife when I entered the shop after having left Huff sitting near a tree in the park across the street. Mrs. Milliner exclaimed loudly that thieves had taken over the city, and she'd take a rolling pin to the next person who tried to touch her.

"Good morning, Mr. Devereux," Mr. Milliner said when he saw me. Mrs. Milliner still wore an indignant frown and busied herself with dusting the spotless counter.

"Good morning Mr. Milliner, Mrs. Milliner. Could you please add three extra rolls and a pastry – one of the fruit-filled ones – to my order?"

"Mrs. Devereux's mother visitin' again?" asked Mrs. Milliner. She must have heard about Lady Grayson from Mrs. Mac, because Valerie almost never left our house when she visited.

I thought about giving Mrs. Milliner something to gossip about, but then I decided to try the truth. Charlie and I had been living a half-lie our entire tenure in this time, and telling even small truths was infinitely appealing.

"Actually, my wife has taken on the services of a pickpocket who robbed me yesterday, and the little thing is half-starved. I imagine she'll be hungry when she comes in to work today."

Mr. Milliner barked out a startled laugh, as though I must be joking, and Mrs. Milliner just stared at me. "Are ye all right, Mr. Devereux. Hit your head during the robbery, did ye?"

I grinned. "I am many things, Mrs. Milliner, but I assure you, that touched in the head is not one of them. There is a saying you may have heard? Keep your friends close and your enemies closer? I didn't appreciate attracting the attentions of a pickpocket, so having one nearby will help to keep me sharp, and therefore less likely to become a target again."

Mrs. Milliner snorted indelicately, and I liked her for it. "First, me cousin gets robbed of his goose, and now me customer hires a thief. The heat has made this city mad."

"I'm very sorry to hear of your cousin's loss, Mrs. Milliner. Perhaps my new employee could be helpful in locating the architect of this deed?"

"I don't know it was an architect – a common thief, more like. A band of 'em actually – gypsy children or the like. Swarmed him, tripped him, and when he dropped the goose to swat the brats, they chased the goose down the street and got away."

"Ah, so it was a live goose. I had wondered."

"A beautiful white thing it were, with three black bands across its tail," she said, as though the beauty of the man's dinner made its loss more dear.

"I will keep my eyes open for any band-tailed geese that might be wandering the city. Thank you for the bread, and I wish you both a good day," I said, after I'd signed the bill for the bag of fresh baked goods.

"Here's for that great beast of yers, Mr. Devereux. Mrs. Devereux buys 'em special." Mr. Milliner handed me a small cookie in the shape of a dog, and I grinned.

"Ah, that explains much. Huff and I thank you for the treat. It will come in handy when we encounter the avian residents of the park, I think."

"Mind ye watch yer silver, Mr. Devereux. I've no notion why ye'd hire a thief, but at least have the sense not to let her alone with yer finery."

"I'll certainly take your warnings in the spirit in which they're intended, Mrs. Milliner. Thank you."

The bell clanged merrily as I closed the door behind me, and Huff waited with great patience for me to cross the street. His tail thumped, and his shaggy face wore a grin as I approached. Huff was a mix of something very large that resembled an Irish wolfhound and a terrier, with the approximate coloring of dust. Gryf, on the other hand, was sleek and black, though equally large and frightening at first glance. The primary danger from each of them however, was that they would knock a man over in their attempts to lick his face, though they never jumped at women or children. Once they'd calmed down, the only concern they presented was the likelihood of tripping over the lazy lumps.

I threw sticks for my beast on the walk home, and rewarded him for not chasing the ducks with the cookie from Milliner's bakery. We both had smiles on our faces as we entered the kitchen door.

Jess sat stock still at the kitchen table. She faced the door with her hands crossed in front of her on the wooden surface. Her shoulders were tense, as though she expected a berating, and her voice carried its familiar defensiveness. "Ye 'ave strange locks," she accused.

"You shouldn't have been able to pick them," I retorted, more sharply than I intended.

"I didn't. I climbed in through a bedroom window. Why don't ye have any furniture?"

I huffed. "You came in through the servants' rooms on the third floor. As you may have surmised, we don't have servants." I was actually angry, and it surprised me. "You could have been killed."

She looked incredulous. "By those beasts? Not likely."

"In a fall. The third floor windows are thirty-five feet up. And my trees are far enough removed from the house to make a jump impossible."

The girl made a dismissive gesture. "Ye live in a semi-detached, for all it's a mansion. Ye may not be easy for the average 'ouse-breaker, but yer neighbors are, and I'm not average."

Amusement was finally beginning to seep past my annoyance, and I busied myself with the bread basket. Jess stood and retrieved three breakfast boards from the cupboard she must have scouted earlier. "Yer lady is awake, by the way."

"Does she know you're here?" I asked as I set out the butter and cheese.

Jess scoffed. "I know better than to startle a lady when 'er man's not at home. I'd just as soon not get a bullet or a knife to the throat if ye please."

I smirked. "Are women that much more dangerous then?" I set the kettle onto the cooker to boil and pulled out three mugs.

"The capable ones are. We don't 'ave size or strength on our side, so we make up for it in brains and quiet." Jess took the rolls from me and sliced them open one by one without denting the crust or dropping more than a few tiny crumbs in the basket. Her hands were scrubbed clean, I saw, though the rest of her still wore a dirt camouflage.

"Was your bed still available last night?" I asked, because it was as safe a topic as I could think of in the moment.

She grimaced. "I 'ad to knock 'Annah out of it to get my things. I let 'er sleep there after I 'ad 'em though."

"Your things were in your bed?" I tried to picture what things this young girl could possibly have that hadn't been stolen from her long ago.

"The beds at St. Marylebone's 'ave little cubbies under the 'ead of 'em. It's where we can keep our own things, and why it makes sense to share a bed with someone ye trust a little. That way, she's sleepin' on the cubby in the day, and ye're sleepin' there at night, and both of ye 'ave a safe place to keep yer treasures."

I'd never lived in a workhouse when I was young, and beds had been few and far between until I made a flat for myself above an accountants' office by the river. The idea that the only way a person had to protect their valuables was to lay their head on them was not the startling one – it was that the workhouse had figured it out too.

41

Charlie's entrance into the kitchen was announced with great pomp and circumstance by Gryf, who danced straight over to Jess and laid his enormous head into her lap. He looked up at her with eyes that should have come with batting lashes. She absently rubbed his ears with one hand as she watched Charlie come in, and I was absurdly pleased that the dogs wouldn't be a problem with our new employee.

I measured the coffee grounds into the pot and added the boiling water. Then I set the press lid on top. Charlie's expression didn't betray one bit of surprise at the sight of a little street rat at our kitchen table.

"Good morning," she said brightly. She came straight to me and kissed me as she always did, unconcerned about the child at our table, then she inhaled the scent of steeping coffee with a sigh. "Ah, lovely. Thank you for making breakfast."

I grinned at her. "I know your secret trick with the dogs. Mr. Milliner betrayed you and your dog cookies."

She arched an eyebrow and gave me a mischievous smile. "You have spent far too much time in the university library, my dear. Your powers of observation are slipping. I've been training the dogs with treats since the moment they arrived." She acknowledged Jess with a smile. "Thank you for slicing the rolls, Jess. You did lovely work."

"How do you know it wasn't me?" I protested.

Charlie's sigh was of the long-suffering variety, and she ignored me. "There's a linen closet on the third floor that I haven't investigated – there was no need before. Perhaps you and I can wash some sheets and make up a proper bed for you?"

I gaped at Charlie. "A proper bed? As opposed to—"

"As opposed to the nest of rugs she slept on last night." Charlie peered at me closely. "Are you quite well, Ringo?"

"I'm quite confused, actually. Jess just got here this morning."

The girl was watching our exchange like it was a tennis match, with eyes wide and mouth firmly shut.

"Did she tell you that?" Charlie plucked a roll out of the basket and buttered it for me, then one for herself.

No, she hadn't told me that. I'd just assumed she had slipped into the house while I was at the bakery. The anger was unaccountably back, and I turned on Jess. "You climbed across the roof and into the third floor in the dark? Are you mad?"

Her expression turned sullen. "I was wrong to stay 'ere, and it'll not 'appen again," she said to the table.

"Don't you see, Jess? He's angry because he's afraid. Afraid you'd be hurt, afraid he'd be powerless to help." Charlie's voice was quiet, calm, and soothing, and it acted like a cool breeze on my temper.

I pushed the press down on the coffee and poured three cups. I added cream to Charlie's, and two sugars with cream to

43

mine and Jess's, then set them on the table. I ran my hand across Charlie's shoulders as I sat next to her on the bench.

"She's right," I said to Jess. "I'm sorry for snapping. I used to climb around rooftops just as high and pitched as our own when I was even smaller than you."

Her face was still sullen, but at least she met my eyes. I added, "It unnerved me that you picked my pocket – I used to be better than that."

Jess turned quickly to Charlie. "I'm sorry fer stealin' yer bob, ma'am. That won't 'appen again neither."

Charlie smiled. "You're forgiven."

"Did ye really earn that yerself?" she asked. "'E said ye did, but 'e could 'ave just been playin' on my sympathy."

"I've sold some of my drawings to a children's book publisher, so yes, I did earn that with my own labor."

I watched Jess as I took a sip of my coffee. I had never broken the habit of too sweet, too creamy, strong coffee – and based on the surprised pleasure on Jess's face when she took a sip, she likely wouldn't either. She studied me, and then the French press I'd made from a piece of cheesecloth and a metal frame. It was based on the classic French press design I'd used in the kitchens at Elian Manor, but which wouldn't be patented until 1929.

"What for makin' coffee is that thing? I've never tasted anythin' like this, not even when Lucy's mum traded me sugar and two quarts of fresh milk for that goose the other day."

I almost spit the coffee I'd just sipped. "A goose? One you just happened to find wandering around London?"

She glared at me. "Yeah. Wot's it to ye?"

I explained to Charlie, "Mrs. Milliner's cousin was very upset to lose a live goose to a band of children who surrounded him. When he dropped the goose to defend himself, they chased it away down the street."

Jess said nothing, and the sullen look was back. I studied her while she neatly avoided my eyes.

"You can't nick from the working class," I said. "They're just a step or three above the street, and sometimes they've even been there themselves. When the street steals from the shops, the bakers and the grocers stop feeling sorry for any of them. They stop handing out bruised peaches and day-old bread when the littlest ones with dirty cheeks come begging at the back door, and they stop giving jobs to the strong or smart ones because a few bad apples have spoiled the whole barrel. The odd goose or jug of milk is just not worth the cost to the whole system."

She glared at me, suddenly angry. "They chase us off and yell for the coppers when they see us lookin' in their bins. If they knew what the street was really like, they wouldn't poison the meat scraps, or leave us potatoes that make us sick."

45

"Green," I murmured under my breath.

"What?" She was fuming, and I realized I'd spoken out loud.

"Green potatoes. They go green when they've been exposed to sunlight, and it makes them toxic ... er, poisonous to eat, especially raw. Cut off the green bits and you'll be okay."

She still glared. "What about the meat then?"

"You can't eat meat that's been thrown out. It'll give you salmonella or E. coli, and if it were still good enough to eat, don't you think the shopkeeper would have had it made into a stew for his family?" I sighed in exasperation. "You imagine they're doing these things *to* you. They're just doing what they do — they throw out meat that's too off to cook, toss out potatoes that have gone toxic. Dogs know better than to eat them — you lot should too."

Jess stood quietly from the table. She held herself very still and looked years older than she was. "Ye're right. We should know better." She looked at Charlie and dipped her eyes. "Ma'am." Then she cleared her dishes to the sink.

"Jess—"

She didn't acknowledge her name and slipped out of the kitchen door, closing it softly behind her.

Chapter 6 – A Purpose

Charlie shook her head at me. "E. coli and salmonella?"

"What street rat doesn't know enough not to eat spoiled meat?"

"A hungry one, or one with others to care for," Charlie said.

I took a sip of my coffee. "Do you think we'll see her again?"

"She's prickly, and proud, and fiercely independent. She has no trust for us, but I do think she wants to, much as I did when you and Saira found me."

I straddled the bench and drew Charlie to me, her back fitted against my chest, my arms around her waist. She leaned her head back to my shoulder, and I inhaled the lilac scent of her hair.

"I've never heard that argument against stealing from the merchants before," she murmured.

"I did quite a lot of reading about the Victorians, as we're called in history books, when I was at Elian Manor. Did you know that just two percent of England's population is the aristocracy? Their ancestors figured out long ago how to avoid taxation, despite controlling most of the country's real estate and much of its wealth. The middle class, including the captains of industry at the upper end and the merchant class like the ones our friend Jess feels targeted by at the lower end, comprise only about fifteen percent of the people, and the rest are the working poor and the poor. The middle class and the working poor endure the vast majority of the tax burden, yet combined, they only own fifty percent of the land."

"That seems grossly unfair," Charlie said as she turned to look at me. "How does one effect change?"

I sighed and ran my hand through my hair. "*We* don't." I said. "I shudder to think what sort of changes we've already accidentally wrought, doing what we do, and knowing what we know."

She searched my face with those glorious, knowing eyes, and I continued. "Yesterday, for example, I went to a luncheon at which, historically, I hadn't been present. Whether one person, more or less, at that table could have changed something significant about the outcome of the meeting, I don't know, but I had to actively bite my tongue to keep from saying anything at all about Sherlock Holmes."

Charlie tried to hide a smile that threatened, but I saw it, and I shook my head at my own dramatics. "And today, telling a street urchin about E. coli? She already mentioned the strange locks, and I'm pretty certain a French press hasn't been invented yet …" I trailed off in disgust at myself. "I'm hiding here. I'm afraid to know what I know in case I say or do what I shouldn't. It's no way to live, Charlie, but I don't know how to do any differently."

She reached out and touched my face, as if to wipe away the tight stress around my eyes and mouth. "My darling, the history that makes the books is written by the victors. The poor never were and never will be victorious in any version of history, and change comes so slowly that individual contributions are always lost in the great gradual tide. So my advice, for what it is worth, is to stop hiding. You have skills and knowledge that can help people, Ringo. Take what you know and make a difference to individual lives, and trust that whatever ripples might be created in the fabric of time can be absorbed. Introducing a French coffee press a few years before someone else invents it won't change history, nor will having a conversation with men over a luncheon. Give yourself permission to participate in our community. In the end, it's our connection with people that matters most to us."

I looked at her a long moment, and heard the echo of her words travel from my ears to my heart. Then I took her face in my hands, and I kissed her with every ounce of my soul. "I love you with all my heart, Charlie Devereux."

She smiled and squeezed my hand. "I love you too. Now let's go upstairs and see what furniture we can move to make proper bedrooms out of the third floor."

"Bedrooms – plural?" I asked.

Charlie turned her deep blue eyes to mine, and said with perfect confidence, "If she returns, she won't be alone."

I laughed out loud. "Dear Mrs. Milliner would have a conniption to learn we've opened a halfway house for orphans."

"They won't be orphans. They'll have us," my very wise wife replied.

CHAPTER 7 – WILDE

Many sweaty hours of dragging furniture out of storerooms, beating the dust from rugs, and making beds with fresh linens, resulted in an upper floor with six serviceable bedrooms. I rigged trundles under each single bed for an additional mattress, and at Charlie's suggestion, added two chests per room, each one fitted with a padlock and key.

We were in the second library organizing books by category as I'd seen future libraries do, when there was a knock at the door. The dogs, of course, went mad, as it was their job to do. That was likely one of the reasons we rarely had guests. My general lack of neighborliness was another.

I fought through the mass of two swirling dogs to answer the door myself. I was wariness and caution itself as I pulled it open to confront whoever had the temerity to visit us.

"Ringo, my good man. Did no one tell you how utterly scandalous it is for one of your obvious means to open his own front door? Unless of course this isn't your house, and then I must ask if your employer is aware that his doorman is wearing shirtsleeves?" Oscar Wilde's enormous grin was actually a welcome sight, and I wondered for a brief moment what, exactly, I'd been afraid of when I'd heard the door knocker.

"Come in, Oscar. Push through the hounds and feel free to join me in shirtsleeves if it is your pleasure to do so, as I will not put on one of those infernal coats in my own home." I opened the door wide and stepped back for him to enter. Oscar Wilde topped me by at least six inches, and his personality took up most of the room, but behind the razor sharp wit and fierce intelligence, lay a generosity of spirit that was as remarkable as it was unexpected.

He also had a storehouse of grandly theatrical gestures which he used to great effect, as he did at this moment when he swept into the entry hall of our home, right past two thunderstruck dogs, and flung his arms around his head at the impossibly large house we'd inherited.

"How does all this wondrous beauty exist for the pleasure of just one man?"

"It exists solely for the pleasure of his wife, who only tolerates the visits of those who appreciate the ridiculousness of its grandiosity," Charlie said with a smile as she entered the hall from the library.

Oscar swept his hat off in a deep, exaggerated bow. "My lady Devereux," he said, rolling his r's with pomposity. "It is my great pleasure to admire this palace of pulchritudinosity, but especially, to gaze in wonder on the beauty and grace of its owner." For that gesture, he merited a swipe of Huff's tongue, which he made a show of wiping off with a grin before he ruffled the dogs' heads.

Charlie laughed and strode forward with both hands extended to him in greeting. "Mr. Wilde, it is our great pleasure to welcome you to our home. My husband told me of his adventures yesterday, and I'm quite delighted that you made good on your threat to call."

Oscar clasped her hands in both of his, then lifted the back of each one to his mouth to kiss. "Devereux, I'm stealing your wife."

I grinned as I led him into the library. "I warn you now, she is absolutely lethal with a frying pan."

Oscar tucked Charlie's arm under his and patted her hand. "So cooking isn't your forte, madam?"

"Actually, a cast iron pan has been used on a blackguard to great and painful effect in my wife's hands," I answered out of turn. "I do believe I'd become her next victim if I so much as joked about letting her leave me." I'd brought him into the finished library rather than the one we had been working in, and he looked around the room with a sigh of appreciation.

"Madam, your husband invited me to remove my coat and join him in his shirtsleeve revolution. If it does not offend your

53

sensibilities, might I do so? I find this among the most welcoming and comfortable rooms in which I've ever had the pleasure to be."

Charlie tilted her head charmingly. "I promise not to run screaming from the room, but only if you will help yourself to whatever you'll have from the bar while I go and make a pot of tea and some properly-sized sandwiches with all their crusts left on."

She kissed my cheek on her way out of the room, her eyes sparkling at me in a way I translated to mean *have fun*.

"My God, man, but you have excellent taste in wives," Oscar exclaimed when she'd gone and the dogs had settled themselves around the room.

"I'd thank you if I thought I had anything to do with her magnificence, but I'll accept the compliment on her behalf."

Oscar had taken off his coat and draped it over the arm of the sofa as he caught sight of one of Charlie's drawings that I'd framed and hung between the windows. It was one of my favorites – a scene from her childhood in Whitechapel, of a fruit seller with his back turned while a small child plucks an apple out of his basket. The child looked quite ordinary, if threadbare and scrawny, until you looked more closely.

Oscar had not seen it until he was right in front of the drawing, and then he exclaimed, "It's a faun!" His expression, when he turned to face me, was like a child who had just learned to whistle.

His gaze returned to the drawing, and he studied the signature. "Charlotte Kelly," he said, his voice full of wonder. "What an extraordinary drawing. May I buy it from you? No, don't answer that. Just tell me where to find Ms. Kelly so I may pester her for my own."

"We have others if you'd like to see them," I said, carefully dodging the question.

"Yes! How dare you keep such magic and wonder to yourself! Lead on, young man!" Oscar's exuberance was contagious, and I led him through the main floor rooms where I'd carefully framed even the smallest of Charlie's drawings.

The wood sprites charmed him, the brownies delighted him, and the fairies – even the nasty ones with expressions of malice and mischief – made him swoon. The trolls and goblins and various beasties would give him nightmares for days, he said. Each drawing was filled with every detail of Victorian London, down to the cobblestone streets and the crackle of flames in the fires by the river. Each drawing also had something mystical, something magical, something *other*, masquerading in human guise.

Charlie had returned to the library with a tray of beautifully unfussy food and a pot of tea with three cups. Oscar was waxing poetic about the remarkable Charlotte Kelly as we walked in, and her startled eyes found mine.

"I must meet this woman, Devereux. You must take me to her at once!"

55

The look of a deer in the headlights passed across Charlie's face almost faster than I could see it before she wiped her expression clear and returned to her usual serene sparkle. Oscar finally noticed her and demanded theatrically, "Do you know the artist of these fantastical drawings, Mrs. Devereux?"

"I do," she said quietly.

"Introduce me!" He took a breath to bring his stage voice back down to something appropriate for polite company. "Forgive me the outburst, madam. I would be ever so grateful if I could meet the artist of the little scenes of wonder. It's as if one could glimpse these mystical creatures around any corner in London, tucked discreetly into the scenery as they are."

Charlie squared her shoulders in a gesture she knew I would interpret correctly, and stepped forward with her hand outstretched. "It's a pleasure to meet you, Mr. Wilde. I was ... am Charlotte Kelly."

I had never actually heard deafening silence before. It was a fascinating thing to experience, as if the molecules of air that moved in the presence of Oscar Wilde – which was all of them – suddenly froze in place and hung suspended in the room around us.

I'd also never heard the big man whisper. "You see them," he said, in a wondrous breath.

Charlie's hesitation was a fraction longer before she gave him a tiny nod. "I do."

Oscar suddenly dropped into the sofa and stared, first at nothing, then at the drawing of the faun child, and then at my wife. "I see glimpses sometimes, as if their true faces peek out at me from behind the glamour. I have sometimes wondered if I am mad."

Her smile, as she poured him tea, was a slow-spreading, quiet thing, but it lit her eyes with warmth. "I don't see the glamour. I only see the true faces."

"Do they know you – know that you can see them?"

She shook her head. "My mother taught me to look away. She said the fauns and the sprites will duck and hide, but the brownies are tricky, the goblins turn nasty, and the fairies will steal away the children who see them."

Delight was slowly replacing Oscar's expression of shock and awe. "And how did your mother know? Could she see them too?"

Charlie shook her head. "She was Irish. They just know."

His smile was wide. "Indeed we do. These *others* inhabit our bedtime stories. They're the fables used to scare wee ones into minding the rules. Very few of us Irish ever lose the habit of believing in magic, for good reason, it seems."

He bit into a sandwich with relish and sighed with contentment. "Might I persuade you to allow me to purchase a drawing or two from you, Mrs. Devereux?"

"You may call me Charlie if you like," she said softly, with a quick glance at me. She didn't need my permission and she knew it, but my smile showed my support.

"Only if you call me Oscar," he also gave me a quick look to determine my comfort with the familiarity. I rolled my eyes to the ceiling in mock suffering.

"You look to me as if anything *I* ever do fits the rules of proper etiquette."

Oscar snorted. "Quite."

Charlie went to the wall and took down the faun child drawing. She handed it to Oscar. "I would be honored if you would accept this as my gift to you, Oscar."

He held it reverently, the gilt frame around the small drawing like a shining bit of gold in his long-fingered hands. "I accept your gift to honor the spirit of generosity in which it was given, and I hope to repay your kindness many times over if you will but give me the opportunity."

He hugged the drawing to his chest before he set it aside on his coat. Then he leaned forward to look at me. "You, however, have created a bit of a mess."

I sighed. "When don't I?"

"What do you know about Conan Doyle?"

I knew this was coming, and I got up and held up one finger. I stepped out of the library and nearly ran down Jess, who stood in the hall, studying one of Charlie's drawings that hung there.

The traitorous dogs hadn't even warned me of her presence, which meant her stealth skills were impressive indeed. Her eyes were huge, but curiously not frightened. I inclined my head to her in greeting, then continued into the other library to retrieve a magazine. When I went back through the hall it was empty, but I left the door to the library open in case she returned.

I held up a three-year-old copy of Beeton's Christmas Annual, with *A Study in Scarlet* emblazoned on the front cover. "I know he is an author of mysteries."

Oscar studied me a long moment. "I believe you may know a bit more than that, but I see no need to pursue that at the moment. Well, after you left yesterday, Stoddart offered Conan Doyle a commission to write for Lippincott's, which Conan Doyle, being no fool, accepted on the spot. Later, he confided in me that he had been struggling to create new and interesting adventures for his characters, Watson and Holmes, and the conversation with you had been the first time since *A Study in Scarlet* was published that he had been excited to go home and write."

I met Charlie's eyes across the low table and winced. She smiled in sympathy and returned her attention to Oscar, who was still speaking. "Now, Conan Doyle has asked me to inquire as to the possibility that he might meet you again, so as to hear more tales of your deductions, logic, and reasoning, as it inspires such interesting possibilities in the plots of his own stories. And—" he

59

held up a hand to forestall the comment I'd been about to make. "And, he wonders if perhaps he could drop his own little mystery into your lap to see what you make of it."

I shot another quick glance at Charlie, but she studied Oscar curiously. "Conan Doyle has his own mystery?"

"Well, not his own, precisely, but one that was handed to him by virtue of his having written this Sherlock character."

He said *this Sherlock character* as if Sherlock Holmes were merely a curiosity, and would not one day become the detective against whom all others were measured.

Oscar continued, including both of us in his gaze. "The wife of a doorman at the Langham, a Mrs. Hartwell, has brought a mystery to Conan Doyle in the hope that he can help her husband, John, who stands accused of a crime she says he did not commit."

I said nothing. The doorman at the Langham had seemed a decent sort, but I didn't know him beyond the exchange of a few words.

Oscar waited for the dramatic gasps of shock and surprise. When none came, he raised an eyebrow and continued in a less theatrical vein. "It seems that a rare and valuable blue carbuncle has been stolen from the hotel suite of the Countess of Morcar — at the Langham Hotel, of course. Apparently, Mr. Hartwell has a criminal record and he had access to the room, therefore he sits in police custody, though no one can produce the stolen item."

"What is a blue carbuncle?" asked Charlie.

I answered automatically. "A carbuncle is another name for a red stone, most often a garnet. In the garnet family there exists a variety of color-changing stones which appears either red or blue, according to the quality of light through which it is viewed. The blue garnet is considered to be the eighth-rarest gemstone in the world, and unlike the color-changing yet small Alexandrite, blue garnets are typically several carats or more in size. The ancient Greeks believed they protected children from drowning and were an antidote to poison, and garnets are noted in the Koran as illuminating the fourth heaven."

Oscar snorted in amusement at my recitation of facts. "This—" he waved airily in my direction. "This is why Conan Doyle needs your help. The sheer volume of knowledge for which you have managed to find storage in that damnably handsome head is staggering."

I clamped my mouth shut, and Oscar laughed at me.

"I'm going to tell Arthur that I've told you the facts of the case as I know them, and you can decide to investigate or not. But understand this, Ringo: you have inspired an author to write. We become like ticks to the muses who inspire us, sucking their blood for sustenance as we hang on for dear life."

I shuddered with mock horror. "That's a delightful image I won't be able to shake for the rest of the day. Thank you for that, Oscar. I am in your debt."

He stood and swept his coat on with theatrical grandiosity, then cradled Charlie's drawing to his chest with one hand as he kissed the back of Charlie's hand with the other. "My dear lady, it has been one of the great pleasures of my life to have made your acquaintance. Please accept my felicitations on your marriage to this rogue, and I thank you again, from the bottom of my cold, bleak heart, for the most generous gift of your magic."

Her answering smile lit up her face. "You have such pretty words for the fierce scoundrel you are reputed to be. How honored I am that you allow me to see the pussycat beneath the scowling lion façade you wear to such great effect."

He grinned. "Ah, would that neither of us were already married, for by your words alone I am half in love with you."

"And half is what you would be should you ever decide to fall the rest of the way," I growled with a barely-suppressed smirk.

I walked Oscar out to the front hall, and he shook my hand warmly. "It has been a most enjoyable visit to your lovely home. I should very much like to come back again if I may?"

"You are welcome any time, Oscar," I said, and meant it.

He held my hand a moment longer in a handshake. "You can trust me, Ringo. A man with my secrets would never betray those of another."

"A wise friend once told me there is something to be said for living out loud. The secrets get rather exhausting," I said, speaking of both of us.

"In another place or another time, perhaps, it would be lovely to, as you say, live out loud."

"The sad thing is," I said as he stepped outside, "no matter the time and place, there will always be someone afraid of the truth. And fear makes people heartless and cruel, which is why we so often stay in our shadows, keeping the truth to ourselves."

Oscar laid a hand on my shoulder as though he would hug me if it weren't so utterly improper. Instead he gave it a grateful squeeze before turning to walk down the steps.

CHAPTER 8 – THE CARBUNCLE

I found Charlie and Jess in the second library shelving books. Charlie had drawn a J, and Jess was looking for all books in a stack that began with that letter. It was an ingenious way to begin teaching the alphabet, and I was tempted to leave them to it, but Jess saw me and scowled. The fact that she didn't want me there made me perversely reluctant to leave.

"Conan Doyle has given us a mystery to solve," I announced to Jess. It wasn't what either of us expected from me, but I tried to pretend I'd meant to say those words.

I hadn't, at least not out loud.

She and Charlie watched me in bewilderment as I casually strolled to the shelves to help with the filing. "A rare blue gemstone has gone missing, and an apparently innocent man is accused of the theft."

Jess's shoulders tensed, and I wondered how many innocents she'd known who'd been sent up for the crimes of hunger and cold.

"You *are* going to help him, aren't you, Ringo?" Charlie asked.

I held open my hands in surrender. "What can I do, Charlie? Unless the stone miraculously appears from thin air, I see very little I can affect. The man's good name is already compromised by a previous crime, and as unjust as it may be, second chances may be possible for a lucky few of us—" I meant myself, but my eyes landed on Jess and she flinched. "But we are by far the exception to the rule."

Charlie looked away, and my heart sank. I should be better than this, I knew. I'd been given so many unexpected gifts in my twenty years that it seemed the height of miserliness to withhold help just because I felt helpless.

"What if ye 'ad the stone?" Jess spoke to the floor, and her hands were clenched into small fists.

"With the stone, the doorman might not hang, but with the story of its recovery, he might be exonerated."

Jess continued to avoid my eyes, but she seemed unable to look away from Charlie's disappointment in me. Finally, she sighed and pulled something out of her pocket, then opened her hand to show me a sparkling blue and purple gemstone the size of a shilling. "Is this it?"

65

I stared at the glittering gem for a long moment, then at her face, which was equal parts nervous and defiant. I couldn't help myself – I burst out laughing at the ridiculousness of the coincidence.

The tight line of Jess's mouth softened just a little as I gestured to the stone. "May I?" I asked. She nodded, and I picked it up with careful fingers and took it to the light of the window. The purple cast changed to brilliant blue with the cold light of the outdoors as I studied the flawless gem.

"It's quite beautiful." I handed the gem back to Jess, who accepted it after a moment's hesitation, surprise written boldly on her face.

She set it down on the table between us. "It came out of the goose."

Well, that was unexpected. I caught Charlie's eye. and she wore the same stunned expression as I knew I did.

"Tell us," my wife said in a soft voice.

"I was goin' to get the goose back after … after what ye said. But my friend Lucy'd given it to 'er mum, who wrung its neck and plucked it for the pot. When she slit it open to gut it, this fell out of … I don't know, somewhere bloody. At first she thought it was a rock and was about to send it into the river – that's where she did the guttin', see? But Lucy saw it sparkle, and she brought it straight to me."

I was thinking furiously, the paths of my thoughts leading in multiple directions at once.

"Why?" I finally said, refocusing my gaze on Jess. "Why did Lucy give you the stone?"

A whole paragraph of denials and snappy comments crossed her expression without a single one being uttered. Her eyes even narrowed once, like she was getting ready to fling an accusation back at me. But in the end she said none of those things.

"Because I told 'er about the toff who gave me work and a bed when I expected the workhouse and a beatin'." She ducked away from my eyes again. "And she knew I'd bring it to ye."

This girl kept surprising me, and I wasn't sure I liked it. My return to Victorian London and my marriage to Charlie had been as unremarkable as one moving into a Regent's Park mansion could hope for, and for more than a year I had literally kept my head down, trying to blend into a populace within which I had never fit. I had hidden myself away at home, or at the university library, and the world had been protected from the knowledge of the future and the past that I held in my head. My life, since our return, had been safe, and dare I say it, predictable.

From the moment she picked my pocket, Jess had been surprising me, and little by little, I felt the complacency and camouflage with which I'd surrounded myself beginning to crack. It was dangerous, and risky, and I wanted to kick through the rest of it and fling the pieces into the fire. I was so *tired* of being safe.

67

I didn't dwell on what it meant that Jess chose to bring me the stone, but focused instead on what to do about it now that she had. "Right. Well, then. We can give it back to the Countess of Morcar directly, and John Hartwell takes his chances, or we can do a little snooping around ourselves to discover what really happened."

Jess winced. "I suppose we can't keep it?"

"You suppose correctly," I said. "First, we need to establish a chain of custody. Describe for me the man from whom the goose was acquired and the circumstances surrounding its liberation."

The sigh was audible, but to the girl's credit, she sat up, closed her eyes for a brief moment, and began. "It was 'ot, same as it's been for weeks, and the baker's sore back made 'im even crankier, walkin' through the park with a wrigglin' goose under one arm as 'e was. 'Is name was 'Enry, 'e was vain despite bein' a bit down on 'is luck, and 'is wife 'ad probably left 'im for one or the other."

I arched my eyebrows up at that information, but Jess ignored the unspoken questions and continued. "The ones already in a mood are the simplest to rile up, see, so it was easy to get in ole 'Enry's way, swarm 'im, trip 'im up a bit, and get 'im to take a swing at Reesy – who dodged it like a born boxer, mind ye – so 'e let go of the goose. It wasn't anythin' at all for little Oliver to chase the great, 'onkin' beast away like it was the best game in town."

My interest had intensified with each word Jess said, and I wanted to pick her description apart, word by word, and piece it back together again so I could see it in my mind. "You determined the sore back because of how the man held himself when he walked, correct?"

"A course," she replied with a snort.

"The vanity?"

"'E was nearsighted, but 'e didn't wear glasses. 'E 'ad 'em, and wore 'em at 'ome, but squinted like anythin' out in public."

"So you either saw the glasses in a pocket, or he still had indentations from them on his face." I said.

Jess nodded and pointed to the bridge of her nose. "Right 'ere. A man gets dents from the nosepiece. And they weren't readin' glasses neither, because 'e couldn't tell the difference between me and Reesy at one point, and believe me, we look nothin' alike."

"And the fact that he was down on his luck? Something in his clothing or footwear?"

"'Is shoes. For all they were good leather, they were fallin' apart at the stitchin' and scuffed. 'E had tried to cover the scuffs with oil, but it's never the same as proper polish."

"And his wife leaving him? Something in his clothing, perhaps?"

She rolled her eyes at me. "'E'd taken 'is weddin' ring off recently – the mark was still there from the sun, and the finger still 'ad a dent. 'E wasn't fat, so it wasn't weight that made 'im take it off, and she 'adn't died, because widowers still wear the ring. No, 'e was angry she'd left; the knuckle was still scratched where 'e'd pulled the ring off in a fit of temper."

"And of course the light dusting of flour that surrounds a man like a halo after a morning spent baking bread gave his profession away," I said, carelessly. "Thanks to your excellent powers of observation, I have a very clear picture of the occurrence of the goose caper, and now we need to know the extent of Henry Baker's involvement in the theft of the countess's carbuncle."

Jess had a strange expression on her face as she studied me. "We?" she finally said.

I looked her straight in the eye. "I believe my wife hired you to work with us. If you are still so inclined, then yes, I would appreciate your assistance."

Out of the corner of my eye I could see Charlie smother a smile as Jess shrugged and stood up, leaving the gem stone where it still sat on the table between us. "Right then. What's next?"

"Will you please put that in the safe for now?" I asked my wife. I directed Jess to leave the room before me.

"What's a safe?" Jess asked as we departed the library.

"A secure place to hide valuables," I said.

Jess scoffed. "I'll believe that when I see it."

I grinned and bet myself she could be into it within a day.

70

CHAPTER 9 – HENRY BAKER

The butcher, whose name, Mr. Cleaver, always made me grin foolishly, had a well-sized goose in his stores of freshly butchered and cleaned poultry. When I showed the package to Jess, she scowled.

"That's bigger than the one we got from the baker," she said, "and it's been cleaned for 'im. I'm not sure 'e deserves it after the 'it 'e tried to get in on Reesy."

"I'm sure you're right. However, in this case, the best way to gather flies is with honey rather than vinegar."

Jess snorted, and I realized she had a fairly impressive repertoire of the noises one expects from an old, corpulent, ill-tempered, bushy-eyebrowed man. "What flies and 'oney 'ave to do with anythin' is even dafter than givin' a grouchy baker more than 'e deserves."

"You'll see."

I left her outside Mrs. Milliner's bakery and went in to speak with my baker's wife about her brother. Mrs. Milliner was delighted to hear that I had tracked down the thieves of her poor brother's goose, and she sent a messenger to fetch him right away. I was pleased to note that Jess, without prearrangement with me, had gone after the messenger boy to follow him.

After ten minutes of listening to Mrs. Milliner describe the aches in her ankles, the sad state of the economy, and the horrible woman with no tolerance for hard times whom her brother had married, I was very relieved to see a small-framed, dapper man stride down the street toward us. His resemblance to a rooster was rather striking, and when he entered the bakery, Jess passed by the window just behind him. She gave a quick nod before she left to let me know this was indeed the man from whom they'd stolen the goose.

"This is my brother Henry now. Henry, this is Mr. Devereux, the man who has found your goose," said Mrs. Milliner effusively. How the woman had any breath left at all after her diatribe on everything that was wrong with the world was one of the great mysteries of the ages.

I shook his hand and noted the missing ring, the squint, and the scuffed shoes.

I debated silence, but his frank up and down appraisal of my wardrobe, rather like he was fitting me for the size of my bank account, made me slightly less polite than I might otherwise have been. "If you removed the lifts from your shoes, sir, you would likely have less pain in your back."

He looked surprised at first, and then he scowled as Mrs. Milliner scolded him. "Henry, you know it's foolish to wear lifts. Da always complained about his back, and Ma swore up and down it was from trying to look taller than he was."

I almost felt sorry for opening my mouth, until Henry snarled at me. "I'll thank you for mindin' your own affairs."

I shrugged, and said mildly, "Suit yourself. Your wife might come back to you if your temper improved, but you'd likely have to stop gambling with household money too."

Now Mrs. Milliner gaped at me, and in my peripheral vision I could see that Jess had slipped inside the bakery and was listening from below the edge of the counter. "And how do you know that about my brother, Mr. Devereux?"

"Well, the bad temper is clearly from the pain in his back. And it's not difficult to spot the new gambler. They assess everyone they meet for their worth, as your brother just did with me, and you'll notice that his fingertips are stained with the heavy, oil-based inks found in the chromolithographic prints of playing cards. Those facts, coupled with the evidence of recent financial trouble and the departure of a wife, would seem to indicate an acquired gaming habit."

I didn't give either of them a chance to reply, as I realized that cleverness with the cocky baker was likely going to get in the

73

way of the information I needed. "Now, all of that conjecture notwithstanding, I have here a butchered and cleaned goose."

I thrust the butcher paper-wrapped package into Henry's arms and continued. "This is not, however, the same goose that was chased out of your arms. I did find the thief and manage to persuade him to return the profits from that goose, with which I purchased this one. I do hope that is a satisfactory end to this business for you?"

Henry the baker stood there, somewhat dumbfounded, a wrapped goose in his hands, and absolutely nothing to say. His sister did not suffer the same condition.

"Well that's just wonderful, Mr. Devereux!" she exclaimed. "However did you find the thieves?"

I waved a hand. "That isn't important. I just hope my solution to the problem of the stolen goose meets with your approval, sir?"

Henry stared down at the package in his hands. "Well, I had rather been wanting to cook that goose last week when my wife … never mind." He returned his gaze at me, surprise and something that looked a bit like shame still written on his face. "It is generous of you to go to the trouble of finding the thieves, young children though they were, and returning a goose to me – an even bigger one than I'd had before, if my arms don't deceive me. Thank you, sir."

He suddenly placed the goose on the counter and sat on a stool. He removed first one shoe, then the other, and pulled substantial lifts out of the insoles of each one before replacing the shoes. Mrs. Milliner glared at him. "Henry! No wonder you've been so irritable. You're in pain!"

"I regret …" he looked at me, and then his sister, and then the ground, "many things," he said with a sigh.

"Oh Henry," said Mrs. Milliner.

"I was wondering," I began, before the scene could turn maudlin, "might you remember where you bought the original goose that the children chased away?"

"Those children—" The baker sounded remorseful.

I interrupted, though not unkindly. "—said the goose fetched a tidy sum from the butcher to whom they sold it, and I wondered from where such a valuable fowl had come?"

"A man named Breckinridge in Covent Garden sold it to me. He'd received a shipment just that day, and I was his first customer, he said. Perhaps you'll find he still has them, as he keeps the live geese in a yard behind his shop."

Jess slipped toward the door, and I made a show of shaking Henry Baker's hand. "Good luck to you, Mr. Baker. Might I suggest that if you were to wear your glasses more often, you'd know when to compliment your wife on such things as a new hairstyle or a pretty smile. I'm told wives like such things, though mine seems to prefer compliments about well-trained dogs and perfectly ugly trolls."

These were the things I loved best about my wife, but I felt no inclination to share the sentiment with Mr. Baker and his sister. I nodded to Mrs. Milliner, my work there done. "Good day, ma'am. Please give my regards to Mr. Milliner."

The door was just closing behind Jess when I reached it. Mrs. Milliner came rushing forward and thrust a bag at me. "Here, Mr. Devereux. For your dogs," she said, with a flustered grin. I thanked her kindly and left the shop feeling as though a bit of honesty might have made a small difference in a man's life.

CHAPTER 10 – COVENT GARDEN

Jess caught up with me as soon as I was out of sight of the baker's shop windows. "I thought ye'd blown yer chance at 'im when the insults came out," she said without preamble.

"I thought I had too."

"Why'd ye do it then?"

I shrugged. "I don't know. I don't think he's a bad man necessarily, but his sister was too absorbed by the drama of it all to pay attention to her brother's problems, so who else would do it?"

Jess snorted – this one more like the huff of a dog than the disdain of an annoyed old man. "Well, 'e didn't know what was inside the goose, did he?"

I shook my head. "He was quite happy to receive the replacement goose, so no, I don't believe he's the one who fed the stone to the poor band-tailed bird. Perhaps Mr. Breckinridge will have more information for us."

The day wasn't nearly as hot as the day before had been, and even in my infernal coat the walk to Covent Garden wasn't brutal. Jess slipped away from time to time, but I didn't question her on her activity, and she didn't volunteer her whereabouts. I did flip her a coin and ask her to buy us each a lemonade. She brought me a large cup and said she'd had hers at the stand. I knew she'd done no such thing, and left half of mine in the glass. "You have the rest," I said when I handed her the glass to run back to the merchant. She scowled at me, but I caught the smile as she downed the rest of the drink. The cost of the second lemonade remained in her pocket, and I thought it would likely end up in the hands of Lucy's mum at the workhouse or wherever she lived.

The girl had the watchfulness of a hound who has finally found a master who doesn't beat it. She wasn't sure of her footing with me though, and she kept a wary distance most of the time. Yet occasionally, when she'd forgotten to be distrustful, she adjusted her stride to mine and began to mimic some of my speech patterns. I had done the same thing when I first arrived back in London with Charlie. I'd been unconsciously speaking like the people around me for so long that it didn't take much for me to fall into the rhythm – and camouflage – of an upper class accent.

"I suppose we should work out your salary," I said when she walked close enough to me that we could speak without being overheard. We stayed to the less-traveled streets, mostly. They were leftover survival habits for me, current ones for her.

"I already did with Mrs. Devereux."

I was silent, hoping for more. "Did it include room and board?" I finally asked.

"It did."

"Anything else?" I asked.

She stopped and turned to face me, her hands planted firmly on her hips. "Do ye want the change back from the lemonade I didn't drink? Is that the reason for yer sudden interest in what I'm bein' paid? If ye must know, the lemonade seller is familiar to me. She 'as two young ones and no man to 'elp feed 'em. I gave 'er the change so she could get the littles some milk."

I stared at her, utterly abashed. Since when had I let something like that slip beneath my notice? I should have seen the lemonade seller's plight and then given her all the money, not just half of it.

Jess glared back at me defiantly, and I finally sighed. "I used to be better at this. Do me a favor Jess, point out the obvious to me if I'm being daft."

Her glare softened slightly, and then finally left altogether. She nodded once, then resumed walking. "Ye surprise me," she said to the street in general.

79

"Sometimes I'm not what I expect either. I suppose we'll both get used to it eventually."

Covent Garden was among my favorite districts in the city. The bustle of merchants and shopkeepers, customers and thieves, made my heart quicken and my senses sharpen. I felt alive in Covent Garden, where no one knew me and very few noticed me. It was a place to blend in with all the color and life and diversity of London.

Jess had melted into the crowd when we'd turned onto Shaftesbury Avenue, and then found me again a few blocks down Neal Street. "Breckinridge is in King's 'Ead Yard. This way." She wound her way through the webbed alleys and walkways, past stalls selling soap filled with lavender, and shops hawking tin pots and clay bowls. There were pubs on every corner and two or three in the middle of each block. Breckinridge's pub backed up to King's Head Yard, and several crates of live geese were locked to the gate.

Breckinridge himself was of the large, scowling variety of pub owner, but with a surprisingly quiet voice. The geese in their crate made such a ruckus it was nearly impossible to hear him.

"Can you tell me about the goose you sold with the barred tail?" I repeated to Mr. Breckinridge.

His scowl deepened, and though his voice was still quiet, it held a menace I would do best not to ignore.

"I'll not discuss barred tails with you or any man. That one over there—" he flung his arm in the direction of a slender man with small, mean eyes who watched us closely, "Ryder, 'e won't leave me alone about the damn things. 'Who'd ye sell the bar-tail goose to?' 'e asks, as though I didn't 'ear 'im the first ten times. Leave off now, before I set my dogs on ye."

The moment my eyes returned to Ryder, he bolted. I'd been half-expecting it, but I was too far away to stop him, so I resigned myself to the chase.

Ryder was clearly familiar with this part of the city, but he didn't have my love for it. His path was straight across Queen Street and down Nottingham Court. When it was clear I was gaining on him on the straightaway, he turned sharply right, down a long back alley that seemed as though it would return to Neal Street. I used to play hide and seek in these tiny back garden plots when I ran with Lizzer's crowd, in the days when I was called Keys and could shimmy up buildings and into second floor windows as a most agile street rat.

I stripped off my coat and hung it on a fence slat before I leapt to a wall and clambered up the back of a two-story brick building, using window ledges and klinker bricks. The roof was slate, and several tiles were already broken, so I picked my way across it with a light step. The roof next door was more substantial and gave me a better view of Ryder's progress across fences and through back gardens.

81

He was heading toward Castle Street, but I could cut him off in the high-walled mercer's yard. I sprinted across the rooftops of another pub and a dry goods shop before dropping down the drainpipe in the corner of the yard in which Ryder would be trapped.

I stepped behind a storage shed and nearly shrieked to find Jess already there, waiting. "Go near the door," she hissed. "I'll drive 'im to ye."

Inexplicably, I did as she said, and it was exactly where I needed to be when he leapt over the wall. Jess calmly stepped out and tripped him, and he went down hard, sending a flurry of doves into the yard around him. I reached him before he could see me, and I pulled him roughly to his feet.

"Wot the bloody 'ell!" He snarled at no one in particular, given that he couldn't see either of us.

I still happened to have my hand on his arm, and I casually twisted it up behind him in the same move I'd done to subdue Jess. It worked as well on a man as it had on a child. Her eyes glittered as she studied the hold, figuring out how to manage it.

"Now see 'ere," Ryder began, but I cut him off.

"We know about the goose and its shiny blue egg." I used the menace on him, and he sagged in my hold. I didn't let go of his arm and relied on my voice to create a perception of authority and compel his compliance. "Was it you who stole it from the countess?"

The man shook his head emphatically. "Not me, no!"

"Shall we let the police pose the same question, Mr. Ryder? I understand that the management at the Langham Hotel has pressured Scotland Yard to make this their highest priority. Lady Morcar is a very important guest." I had no idea if that was true or not, but it sounded reasonable to my ears, and it certainly seemed to inspire the man.

"It were Catherine – Catherine Cusack, the countess's maid. She slipped the rock to me to take it away from the Langham, while I made sure the coppers knew about Hartwell's record."

"And the goose?" I prompted, still using the menace, and still not allowing Ryder to get a good look at me.

"I got nervous Hartwell would remember me and tell the coppers 'bout my bein' there the same day the rock went missin'. I left word for Catherine and then hid at my sister's farm, but then I worried the coppers would find the note and come for me, so I fed the rock to the bar-tailed goose and asked Sophie to let me 'ave it. Problem was, I didn't know she 'ad two bar-tails, and the one I took was the wrong one. *My* bar-tail she sold to Breckinridge before I could collect it."

I met Jess's eyes behind Ryder's back. The man was trembling and had sung like a bird. I arched a questioning eyebrow at her, and she scanned him quickly with her gaze. She seemed to come to the same conclusion I had, and she nodded once and stepped back out of range of his sight.

83

"Well, Mr. Ryder, what do you suggest I do with you? Mr. Hartwell is clearly innocent of any crime."

"It was on my word he was bein' held. I'm what said I'd seen him come out of the countess's room, and I won't say nothin'. I'll disappear and the coppers'll never find me again, I swear."

"And Catherine?"

"She'll not say a word. I'll tell her to leave her post and disappear, maybe even with me if I can convince her to. She were goin' to pay me for my part, but I'll refuse the money if she comes with me. She's a good girl, that Catherine, bright as a penny. We was just tryin' to do things the easy way, but it's not, is it?" The man was nearly frantic with fear, and it was starting to make my skin crawl. I used my deepest, most menacing voice and spoke directly in his ear.

"Never. Steal. Again."

I pushed him forward, and he stumbled to get his balance. By the time he had turned to look behind him, Jess and I had disappeared into the shadows of the yard.

Chapter 11 – Irregulars

Jess disappeared as we left Covent Garden, and I didn't have great hopes of seeing her for the rest of the day. I wished I could run home, but it was full daylight still, and unless a man is chasing a thief, there's very little reason for him to run through London.

It took several blocks for the adrenaline of the chase and the sick feeling of having deliberately intimidated another man to leave me. There was a bit of exhilaration too – we had solved two mysteries that day, and yet no one would be the wiser. The case against Mr. Hartwell would fall apart with no witness to testify against him, the countess would receive her gem back, and a Mr. Ryder and Ms. Cusack would quietly leave London and their life of opportunistic crime behind. There might even be the possibility of a reconciliation for Mr. Baker and his wife, if the planets aligned perfectly and he groveled with proper humility. But none of these things would be linked back to a conversation between a young man and a thieving girl about a goose, a baker, and a blue egg.

Gryf and Huff met me at the garden gate with all the enthusiasm of long lost friends reunited, and I spent a few minutes wrestling with them on the grass under a big maple tree. Huff finally collapsed on my chest while Gryf lay near my head and obligingly swiped his tongue up my face. I pushed them off me when I heard footsteps coming up the garden path.

"Did you find your thief?" Charlie asked in her quiet, lovely voice.

"Which one?" I rolled over on my side to watch my wife as she sat next to Gryf and ruffled her hands through his fur. He wriggled onto his back and gave two half-hearted thumps of the tail before sinking into a blissful coma of belly rubs.

"The other one. Did you misplace yours?" she asked.

I shrugged. "Jess disappeared after we caught the carbuncle accomplice. The actual thief was the countess's maid, but neither she nor her accomplice will be heard from again."

Charlie studied the belly she scrubbed for a long moment before meeting my eyes. "Hi honey, how was your day?" She giggled mischievously, and then shrieked when I grabbed her waist and brought her down against my chest.

"Did you save any of those little cocktail dresses from Elian Manor, because you suddenly sound very much like a 1950s American housewife."

86

She rested her head against my chest as the dogs arranged themselves on her skirts to pin her in place. She propped her head on her hands and looked into my eyes. "Are you glad we came back to our time, or would you rather be in a place and time where you can take computers apart and play video games with other young men your age?"

I traced her cheekbone with my fingertip. "I'd rather be any place you are, Charlotte Kelly Devereux."

A throat cleared near the garden gate, and Charlie and I looked up from our dog pile on the grass. Jess stood there, a satchel over one shoulder and a paper-wrapped package in hand. Three children of various ages and sizes were arrayed behind her. "I brought some friends for dinner. I thought we'd have goose." She held up the package, and then she smiled.

I didn't ask where the goose had come from, and Jess didn't tell me. She watched carefully as Charlie and Mrs. Mac rubbed the goose with the zest of lemons and limes, salt, and spices, then stuffed it with the zested fruit and springs of parsley, thyme, and rosemary. They pricked the skin of the legs for the fat to render, then drizzled honey on the skin and roasted it for an hour.

Jess tasted a spoonful of the honey and declared it would definitely catch many more flies than vinegar ever would.

We were introduced to her friends as Mr. and Mrs. Devereux. "Ye can call them 'sir' and 'ma'am,' but only 'cause they 'aven't got titles," Jess told them somberly. Reesy was a boy about her age, but large-boned and strong. She trusted him, and he worshipped her and did whatever she asked without question. Hannah was the girl with whom she shared the bed at the workhouse. Hannah didn't speak – not that she couldn't, Jess said, just that she didn't. Occasionally Hannah signed a question to Jess, who understood the odd signals and answered them with whispers. Oliver was the smallest six-year-old I had ever met. He asked questions about everything, and he spoke like a child twice his age. But when he closed his mouth and said nothing, he could have passed for a baby just out of diapers. Charlie caught me behind a door and told me that Oliver was part fae, but that none of the other children knew it. She quickly sketched his true face for me, with long, pointed ears and huge eyes, and then later, made a point of kissing the top of his head when he passed us by.

Mrs. Mac went home, and as the goose was still in the oven, Charlie took the girls to bathe, and I took the boys to the yard to help me wash the dogs. The end result of our efforts was the same, and all four children were clean and hungry when we returned to the kitchen.

For the first time ever, Charlie and I sat on either end of the kitchen table as though we were responsible adults presiding over a feast for children. They were careful to watch how we ate, and more than once Jess shot a glare at Reesy when he forgot to use his knife and fork on the goose.

We determined that none of the children knew their parents, and all had been living either on the street or, when they'd been caught, in St. Marylebone's workhouse or in the Home for Lads just off Paddington and the Grotto Passage. Hannah had been taught her letters there when it was still a Ragged School, but it had closed down with the new education reforms, so the teaching had stopped too.

Charlie's gaze narrowed. "They closed the Ragged and Industrial School in Marylebone?"

Jess shrugged. "No one stayed past age six or seven, 'cause the street kids would beat ye for puttin' on airs."

"Hmph." Charlie met my eyes across the table, and I could literally see the wheels spinning in her brain.

After dinner we retired to the library where I regaled my wife with the account of our adventure of the blue carbuncle. Jess added only a few points for clarity, but otherwise remained mostly silent until I got to the part about letting Ryder go.

"Aren't ye afraid 'e'll steal again now that 'e got away with it?" she asked.

"There's always that chance, of course. But in my experience, especially for a man so predisposed to fear, jail would make him angry and hard, and London would have a much bigger problem on their hands when he got free."

"What does that mean, 'predisposed to fear'?" she asked.

"A predisposition is a tendency toward an attitude or action. In Ryder's case, he tried to make us afraid with menacing looks when badgering Breckinridge for information about the goose got him nowhere. Then we caught him, and a deep voice and an armlock were enough to make him unaccountably afraid. A person who lives their life in such fear will not see reason. They see only threats, and they will either run, or they'll fight. In jail there is no chance to run, so someone like Ryder can only fight."

"And then he comes out with the 'abit of it," Jess said.

"Exactly."

Jess opened her satchel and withdrew a stack of books – my books – that I'd hidden in Regent's Park after she'd picked my pocket. I'd thought them long-since sold, and therefore pointless to ask about. She returned them to me solemnly.

"I'd like to learn to read these … please."

I opened the one on the top, an English translation of the third edition of the *Philosophiae Naturalis Principia Mathematica* by Sir Isaac Newton, and found a page of text without mathematical formulae. "Find the J," I said.

She pointed to one unerringly.

"It's the first letter of your name."

She stared at it as she tried the letter out on her tongue. Then she looked up at me with shining eyes. "J for Jammy. J for Jack-a-dandy. J for Johnny 'Orner?"

I started at the words she chose and again wondered at the experiences this mite of a thing had behind her. Jammy was the height of perfection for young girls, Jack-a-dandy was brandy, and a Johnny Horner was the pub around the corner. I chuckled with chagrin and pointed out the rest of the letters in her name. "We'll work on more tomorrow after we take the stone back to the countess," I finally said, after doing the same for each child.

There was a look of pure triumph on Jess's face, and I wasn't sure if it was because she was learning to read, or because I'd said "we."

My wife shooed all the children upstairs where she put the girls to bed in one room and the boys in another, with a goodnight kiss and a dog in each bedroom for company.

I was reading the *Principia* when she came to bed. "Do you know," I began as she snuggled in beside me and laid her head on my chest, "Newton first published this in 1687? Not only did he invent calculus, but he wrote the four Rules of Reasoning in Philosophy. His four rules revolutionized the investigation of natural phenomena and essentially put the world's unsolved mysteries within the sights of scientists for centuries to come."

I looked down at her and she met my eyes. "There were no computers or video games then, just as there are none now. It was the quest for knowledge – to *understand* – that fueled a man like Newton and gave him inspiration."

Charlie's gaze was intent. "You can do revolutionary things, Ringo – things that are being discovered right now, and even the ideas still to come. You can do that here, in our home, with our band of irregular misfits—"

I laughed. "Irregular misfits?"

"Well, they're hardly regular misfits, as it is merely circumstance that keeps them from fitting in. Staying here with us may not change their desire to blend in with society, but it'll certainly change their ability to."

"A band of irregular misfits. It sounds like the sort of group to which I could belong."

She smiled up at me. "It's the sort of group you lead, with me in the wings to ask the right questions. You especially need me to spot the *others* along the way."

I groaned. "Because the normal human thieves, brigands, and cutthroats aren't bad enough?"

She laughed and kissed me. "Normal is boring."

CHAPTER 12 – THE RETURN

John Hartwell was at his post at the front door of the Langham Hotel when Jess and I arrived. Jess stayed several steps behind me and was dressed in reputably clean clothes and shoes with socks. She was able to slip into the hotel unnoticed while I engaged him in conversation.

"Congratulations on your reinstatement," I said in a casual tone, as though the doorman and I were old friends.

"Thank ye. The coppers got a letter from a prominent citizen sayin' the man who fingered me for the crime had disappeared, so there was none to testify against me. With no evidence, they had to let me go, and I don't mind tellin' ye, makin' even one mistake can follow a man for the rest of 'is life."

I clapped him on the shoulder. "Good luck to you, Mr. Hartwell. I'm glad things worked out." I took note of a fine carriage approaching the hotel and stepped toward the door. "Might you be able to point me to the bellhop's desk?"

"Of course, sir." He directed me to a discreetly placed desk just inside the entrance. Behind the desk was a closet in which I was reasonably sure bellhop uniforms were stored. The bellman at the desk was an ambitious fellow if his watch and shoe shine were to be believed, with a magnificent mustache and a discerning eye for men's fashion. I nodded to the glass doors, through which a footman could be seen lowering the carriage steps.

"Hartwell will be needing your help with the Marchioness's bags. I understand she's an excellent tipper." I had dropped my voice to the level of a confidence and winked at the bellman. His eyes darted to the view of a grand lady descending the steps, and he twirled his waxed mustache grandly.

"Won't you excuse me just a moment, sir," he said, barely glancing at me in his haste to get outside, and taking no note of Jess at all as she emerged from behind a potted plant and tucked herself into the closet.

Less than thirty seconds later she came out wearing a bellboy's cap and a too-large jacket.

"Wait," I said quietly, pulling her into the shadows behind the doors. I rolled the sleeves of the jacket under at her wrists and buttoned it closed.

"Just deliver the order for the countess's tea service and stand clear so they forget you're there," I said quietly. "Make sure it's her own service though." It was common for the aristocracy to keep a set of their own china in the butler's pantry of a fine hotel such as the Langham, so that meals served to them from the hotel kitchens had all the elegance of their private home.

Jess nodded impatiently and twisted out of my hands. She didn't need me to remind her of details we'd thoroughly discussed, but I was afraid for her nonetheless. It was a sensation that sat uncomfortably in my stomach like gelatinous soup.

I watched her stride confidently into the kitchen, and then glanced around the hotel lobby for something on which to focus my attention while I waited. A man and his wife had just arrived at the Langham from a shopping trip to Paris, as evidenced by the tie of his cravat, the startling Parisian pink of the feathers in her hat, and the number of trunks the bellhops struggled to carry. A university student, just back from Cambridge, strolled across the room to greet his parents. The father's impatience and the mother's recent illness went unnoticed by the young man in his trepidation – most likely about his performance at school, if the slovenly condition of his coat and the swollen look of too much drink were any indication.

A glimpse of startlingly red hair down the back of a young woman of modest means and recent bereavement nearly distracted my attention from the kitchen door. A waiter in a room service uniform had emerged, carrying a platter with a teapot and two upturned cups on saucers. I stepped closer and focused on the faint sound of something rattling in the empty pot. I worried it was loud enough to draw the waiter's attention when I saw the redheaded woman turn toward the waiter with a start of surprise, but Jess's reappearance from the kitchen minus the bellhop's uniform, no doubt left discreetly on a baker's rack, refocused my attention on the mission at hand. Jess's stealth as she trailed after the waiter up the staircase gave me the confidence that the countess's carbuncle would be returned to her in her own teapot without incident.

"Ringo! There you are," boomed the unmistakable voice of Oscar Wilde from the door to the restaurant. "We've been waiting for hours," he complained dramatically.

"You've been waiting for less than five minutes," I said, relaxing into a smile as I approached the table where Conan Doyle already sat. "Your tea is still steaming." I had agreed to meet the gentlemen for tea as a cover for returning the carbuncle, and now that the deed was done, I felt free to enjoy their company.

Conan Doyle stood to grip my hand as Oscar shook his head in mock disgust.

"How does your spectacular wife allow you out of the house in such a boring cravat?" he asked, looking pointedly at my very reasonable, very constricting forest green silk.

Conan Doyle barked a laugh. "And what is the excuse for yours then?" He raised an eyebrow at the fanciful paisley coat

Oscar had worn with an embroidered vest – a costume on anyone else, but it suited him perfectly.

Oscar made a grandly dismissive gesture. "If I am occasionally a little overdressed, I make up for it by being immensely over-educated."

When laughter had died down, food had been ordered, and small talk dispensed with, Conan Doyle got to the business of the meeting.

"I did what you asked and made a call to Scotland Yard regarding Mr. Hartwell. Now what do you have for me?"

I looked beyond the dining room to the lobby where Jess again lurked behind the potted palm with which she'd become so familiar. She gave me a discreet nod, and I felt the last tension leave my body. The waiter Jess had followed hurried back to the kitchen, his tray empty and his expression bloodless and frantic. "Well, gentlemen, I believe there will soon be a small disturbance in the butler's pantry."

They both turned, despite being unable to see the door to the kitchens from our table. A moment later a man shouted, a woman shrieked, and the clatter of dishes filled the air. I didn't bother to hide my smile as Conan Doyle and Oscar returned stunned gazes to me.

"What on earth was that all about?" Oscar exclaimed.

"The Countess of Morcar appears to have found her blue carbuncle in her own tea service, where it undoubtedly fell the last time she used it."

Conan Doyle gaped at me, and Oscar whooped in triumph. "You did it!" he cheered. "Well done!"

Several patrons at other tables cast disapproving scowls in our direction, which the three of us roundly ignored. "Tell us how, and don't leave anything out," insisted Conan Doyle.

I did leave out one or two details, but nothing of any real importance to the story. When I had finished my tale and the excellent chocolate soufflé, Conan Doyle declared that Oscar may not steal my life for his work because *he* would be doing so. Oscar merely smiled, as if that had been his intention all along.

We stood to go, and Conan Doyle shook my hand heartily. "I do hope you'll be good enough to meet with me the next time something interesting comes up. I find your powers of deduction to be quite fascinating indeed," he said in his rolling Scottish burr.

I registered Oscar's barely concealed smirk as another flash of red hair caught my eye. I turned to discover if I could see the face to which it belonged and glimpsed merely the swish of a long gray skirt turning a corner as the young woman vanished from sight. Even as I resolved to ask John Hartwell about the red-headed woman, I replied to Conan Doyle without thinking. "I'm sure there are more mysteries in London than just the missing blue carbuncle."

Oscar walked out of the Langham with me, tipping his hat to the bemused Mr. Hartwell at the door. "Ringo, I already knew you had fascinating friends, but I had no idea you would turn out to be so very interesting yourself."

I grinned and raised an eyebrow. "Didn't you?"

"Well," he grinned, "come to think of it, perhaps I did. Your friend Saira was the beautiful girl who could travel through time, and Tom, the tortured soul who believed he was evil, yet it is Ringo, a reformed thief and man of my own time, who remains the greatest mystery of them all."

I laughed. "Stick around, Oscar, there's sure to be more to come."

He and I parted ways at Portland Place, and I continued north toward Regent's Park. A city block later, Jess fell into step beside me.

"Do ye want to run?" she asked.

"Not in this heat, with a too-tight coat and this cravat that is just tame enough that I'd rather not cover it in sweat stains."

She held up my coin purse and dangled it carelessly from two fingers. "Not even for this?" she taunted, right before she took off at a full sprint down the street.

I huffed the sort of dramatic sigh that would have made Oscar proud, and then I took off running.

Chapter 13 – The Pawnbroker

The path Jess chose took us across Marylebone and wound through several passages I'd never before discovered. When Charlie and I first settled here I had studied the history of the village that sprang up on the banks of the Tyburn River. In 1400, the old Tyburn Church was pulled down and a new one built on the top of what is now Marylebone High Street. The new church was named St. Mary's, and the area became known by a French flourish as St. Mary-la-Bourne. The Tyburn Manor changed hands several times until Henry VIII managed to persuade the owners to exchange it for farmland elsewhere so he could build a hunting lodge close to London. The fields and woods became a royal park that has been called Regent's Park ever since.

Marylebone became home to London's wealthy elite, but there remained pockets of extreme poverty tucked between the gracious townhomes. The St. Marylebone Workhouse was built for that reason in the late 1700s, and on our way up to Grotto Passage we passed the Ossington Buildings estate, an answer to low-income housing which was currently under construction in a former miserable slum.

As we approached the Home for Lads, now housed in the old Ragged School building, Jess slowed and slipped into stride next to me. "I want ye to meet someone," she said quietly.

"A friend?" I asked.

"Yeah. Lucy's mum. She doesn't like that I know ye."

So, someone actually was watching out for Jess. "Lead on," I told her.

Jess surprised me with a sharp left turn at Paddington Street. There, on the corner, hung three gold balls – the universal sign of a pawnshop, which originated sometime in the Middle Ages, probably with the Medici family who were pawnbrokers to the popes. This pawnshop looked cleaner than most, and when Jess pushed open the door, a tiny silver bell above it announced our entrance.

The shop was surprisingly well-filled with a startling collection of tools and household implements, jewelry in the case, a few books, some musical instruments, and a variety of what looked like medical scalpels and clamps. My eyes were instantly drawn to the microscope on a high shelf which looked remarkably similar to the brass one that had belonged to Saira's father.

A woman came out of the back wearing a distracted air and a smudge of dirt on one cheek. She was no taller than Charlie and had the physique of someone who had done hard labor in her life. Her hands and the lines on her face made her appear ten years older than she likely was, but when her eyes lit up at the sight of Jess, those years fell away in an instant.

"Ye're clean and fed, and ye look right respectable in those fancy togs," she said to my small companion.

Jess had a swaggery grin on her face as she shoved a thumb in my direction. "It's 'is fault – the clothes anyway. The food and clean's due to 'is missus."

The woman, whom I assumed was 'Lucy's mum,' lost all the smile from her eyes as she shifted a very probing gaze to me. "And ye be ...?"

I opened my mouth to answer, but Jess rushed to fill the gap. "'E's the toff who's teachin' me and the others to read."

I couldn't help the scoff at Jess as I held my hand out to shake the woman's. "The toff's name is Ringo Devereux, and I'm pleased to meet you, ma'am."

She narrowed her eyes as she shook my hand, but her lip twitched, and she might have smiled if she hadn't been so determined to put me in my place. "Georgeann Dorne."

"Mrs. Dorne was the one who found the blue egg in our goose," Jess said to me before she turned to Mrs. Dorne. "And 'e's the one who figured out who nicked it. I took it back today, and didn't the countess make a right fuss!" Jess chuckled proudly.

"Did ye get a reward?" Mrs. Dorne asked suspiciously.

Jess looked surprised and turned her gaze to me. "Did we?"

I sighed. "Unless we wanted the whole tale, from your theft of the goose to the take-down in Camden Market, to be placed before Scotland Yard, I judged it best for the gem's return to remain anonymous."

Mrs. Dorne scowled at me. "'Ow do ye expect the chit to get on 'er feet if ye pull the rug out?"

"I'll be fine. I always am," said Jess defensively.

"'Ow long till ye end up in irons, pickin' pockets of the likes of 'im?" Mrs. Dorne groused back.

My gaze wandered around the small pawnshop, which, on second and third glance, was filled with even more remarkable items than I'd originally realized.

There was a treadle sewing machine set against a wall, almost as though a stool could be brought out and a person could sew right there. Several gas lanterns of different shapes and sizes stood on spindly-legged tables that were set with lace doilies as though the only thing missing was a tea set. Two tea services and three sets of good silver rested in a glass case near the counter, and several lovely teapots lined a shelf. There were hairpins and tortoise shell combs, bone-handled scissors and even two ivory pipes. Everything was clean, well-ordered, and very neatly displayed, as though the shop were a fine house or a museum to life in the nineteenth century.

"How did you come to know Jess?" I asked Mrs. Dorne.

Jess opened her mouth to speak, but I shot her a warning glance. I cared less about the answer than about what this woman chose to say.

"My daughter took to 'er like fleas on a dog. When I couldn't keep 'em apart, I made sure bein' together caused no 'arm."

"And the girls met in ... school?" I asked as innocently as I could manage.

Mrs. Dorne studied me. She knew what I was after, and I could see the moment she warily surrendered the part of her story she hadn't wanted to tell. "Lucy and me, we stayed a spell in the workhouse, just 'til I could get enough saved to pay the rent on this place."

"And now you're living here, in the shop, loaning money to the wealthy women of Marylebone so Lucy can go to school."

Mrs. Dorne shot me a loaded glare. "Ye presume too much, sir."

"But I'm not wrong, am I?" I scanned the beautifully displayed contents of the crowded room. "The things in this shop are primarily the household devices, decorations, and implements used by women. Your shop is clean – far cleaner than any other pawnshop I've ever visited – and you are female. These two things in particular would recommend you to any woman of means in need of cash for which they'd rather not ask husbands, fathers, or men in general."

Jess smirked at the look of speculation on Mrs. Dorne's face. "What else do ye see?" Jess asked me in a cheeky tone, just to stir the pot a little more.

I decided to give in to her question to satisfy my own curiosity, though I was far more interested in what I didn't see, namely, the means by which Mrs. Dorne was able to secure the seed money for her initial loans. It was one thing to rent the space for a pawnshop, but quite another to fund it. I strolled around the room, looking at the prices marked on particular items. "It is interesting to me is that you have two pricing tiers."

I pointed to the two tea sets. One was Doulton & Co. stoneware, and one was a painted Royal Worcester porcelain set. "The Worcester is marked to just ten percent less than retail, which means you likely charged forty percent interest on the loan. It came from a well-to-do household, and the woman likely just bought a new set rather than pay you back for this one. The stoneware set is much more likely to have come from a working class household, and its price is considerably less than retail. That would indicate to me that you are offering loans of half their worth and charging the women who bring in such serviceable items a mere ten percent interest."

I walked over to the shelf that held the microscope and studied the fine brass carefully. Mrs. Dorne stood very still and seemed to barely breathe as I examined it. "I believe, Mrs. Dorne, that a doctor of your acquaintance either died or was beholden to you in some way."

She exhaled, but only because holding her breath would have been conspicuous. I continued as though I hadn't noticed. She was not raised to be an educated woman, as evidenced by her speech, and her hands showed the age and wear of one who has labored domestically. It made her accomplishments that much more remarkable. "You have a head for numbers, and enough learning to understand the running of a business. That would lead me to believe that you did the books for a doctor's household, which may have ultimately led to managing the books for his business as well."

"Why a doctor?" asked Jess. She couldn't see the tight-lipped expression on Mrs. Dorne's face.

I answered Jess directly. "The microscope is a Ross binocular type, circa 1870. It was the premier brand twenty years ago and remains quite valuable. Also, the medical tools in the case over there are very fine, and they are encased in leather with the initials WD embossed on the cover in gold. Female doctors are so rare, and their education is so hard-won, that they're unlikely to ever pawn the tools of their trade, which leads me to the presumption that WD was a male medical doctor." What I didn't say, and what Mrs. Dorne no doubt heard in my silence, was the question of why an educated man would pawn his very valuable implements in a shop owned by a woman and frequented by women.

Jess turned her gaze to her friend's mother and waited. Perhaps she was learning to hold her tongue and let others speak first after all.

Mrs. Dorne said nothing, though her lips thinned to the point of invisibility.

I continued examining the microscope blithely, as though unaware of the electric charge in the air. I was left with two assumptions. One – theft, or two – blackmail. I masked my study of Mrs. Dorne with another turn about the room as I pondered the question. Theft was unlikely, as success in the pawnbrokering business was predicated on trustworthiness, and if the doctor's items had been stolen, he or his family could ruin Mrs. Dorne's business and her name, which were essentially the same thing. It had not gone unnoticed by me that the pawnshop's name was G. Dorne Ltd.

I smiled at Mrs. Dorne, and she narrowed her eyes as though she could hear the direction my thoughts had taken. Jess looked back and forth between us with an expression that danced between amusement and concern at the charged silence between us.

"I admit I'm curious as to how you came to possess such a unique medical instrument in a pawnshop that appears to contain the worldly goods of women." My eyes rested casually on Mrs.

107

Dorne's face as I said this, but her hands gave away her distress as she gripped the sides of the counter hard enough to whiten her knuckles.

I allowed my gaze to soften, and I smiled at Mrs. Dorne. The woman standing before me was a kind woman under all her suspicion and secrets. She had cared for Jess when perhaps no one else would, and I didn't need to expose the fact that the doctor was likely Lucy's father.

The hands that had clenched the counter were forcibly spread open as Mrs. Dorne inhaled deeply and let out a long slow breath.

"What do you imply with your speculation, Mr. Devereux?" Her voice was even, though I could see the effort it cost her to make it so.

"Nothing, Mrs. Dorne. Nothing at all. I was merely curious if, perhaps, the Ross microscope might actually be for sale."

She watched me for a long moment, evidently making up her mind that whatever threats might be associated with me were not immediate. "It 'appens the owner of the microscope died recently, and the claim ticket for 'is tools seems to 'ave gone missin' from 'is estate."

"Ah, indeed. Then I should like to offer your asking price, plus fifty percent," I said.

Two sets of eyes widened in surprise at my words, but I continued before either could speak. "Consider it an investment, if you will," I casually eyed the price tag on the battered pedal-powered sewing machine, "to cover the cost of returning this to its owner. I am correct in assuming it was a down-on-her-luck seamstress who pawned this machine?"

"'Twere," Mrs. Dorne said. "I'm 'oldin' it until 'er 'usband gets more work. She's doin' her sewin' by 'and 'til then."

I nodded. "If you would be so kind as to see that the seamstress has her tools-of-the-trade returned to her, I would appreciate it."

Mrs. Dorne studied me carefully. "Why are ye doin' this, Mr. Devereux?"

"To gain your trust," I said simply.

"With Jess?"

My tone remained casual, but I didn't look away from her gaze as I spoke. "There was a time, not too long ago, when wits and luck were all I had. I see a bit of that in Jess too, and something else. Her ability to trust other people hasn't been beaten out of her by the difficulty of surviving alone. That tells me she's had people to watch her back. It says something about her that she allows it, and it says something about the people she's let herself trust. You are one of those people, Mrs. Dorne, and watching a child's back as they make their way forward in the world is one of the most worthwhile things a person can do. You are an admirable woman."

Mrs. Dorne looked away and seemed very interested in an invisible smudge on a shelf behind her. I made a point of studying several books stacked on a table while she took a couple of deep breaths. Finally, she exhaled sharply and turned back to me with unmistakably shiny eyes. The line of her mouth was still grim and unsmiling, but something had softened in her expression. She cleared her throat and nodded perfunctorily.

"Will ye take the scope with ye today or pick it up later?"

I counted out the correct amount of money and placed it on the counter. "I'll take it now if you have something to wrap it in."

"I do." She pulled a long strip of waxed canvas out of a box and wound it around the microscope, then packed it into a basket and handed it to me.

"Mrs. Bowers will thank ye for the return of 'er sewing machine," she said, not ungraciously.

I felt the fabric which encased the microscope. "Do you have more of this material, Mrs. Dorne?"

She nodded. "I 'ave a bolt in the back."

"Would you be so kind as to ask Mrs. Bowers to make a satchel from this material for me – something big enough to hold four or five books ..." I demonstrated with my hands "... with a leather strap long enough to sling across my chest?"

"I 'ave the right needles for 'er sewin' machine, so I don't see it would be a problem."

"I thank you, Mrs. Dorne. I will, of course, pay for the materials, for Mrs. Bowers' time, and a commission to you for relaying my request."

Mrs. Dorne nodded with a look of surprise. "Then I'll add my thanks to ye as well."

I bowed to her as I took my leave. "I expect I will see you again, Mrs. Dorne. Good day."

Chapter 14 – A Business Plan

Jess stayed behind a moment after I'd left the pawnshop, and she caught up to me as I entered the park. I took the long way home because my brain worked more effectively when I was in motion, and perhaps unbeknownst to her, Mrs. Dorne had given me some things to think about.

"She's afraid ye want somethin' from me," Jess said, with no preamble. I'd been listening for her this time, so she didn't startle me.

"Maybe I do."

She snorted in derision. "Ye're not the type."

I scoffed in return. "The predatory type? You and I have both spent enough time on the street to know they're just as likely to be gentlemen as dock workers – possibly more likely, given all the rules and strictures by which gentlemen have to pretend to live."

She laughed. "Ye're foolin' yerself if ye think the – what'd ye call 'em? Predatory?" She pondered the word a moment, and nodded as though deciding it fit. "Ye're mad if ye think the predators are in it for the rule-breakin' bit."

I found myself intrigued as to her theories, and concerned about how she arrived at them. "Enlighten me then."

She shrugged. "We look out for the blokes that are afraid, like a dog that's been kicked too many times and then learns to bite the 'and before it can cuff 'im. We learn to smell the fear before it can get close enough to 'urt, and we stay away from the ones who feel big only when everyone else around them is made small. It's mostly blokes, maybe because everyone expects 'em to be so strong, but sometimes it's ladies too. They're even more dangerous because a person never even sees the knife before they're pullin' it out of their back. At least with blokes it's physical – they can 'urt yer body, but they can't get yer mind if ye don't let 'em."

I studied the girl who walked beside me as I marveled at her insightfulness. I began to wonder in earnest about where and who she came from. She was small-boned, with musculature that made her slender rather than skinny. Due to her bath the night before, her black hair was clean, if still raggedly cut, and in the new delivery boy suit she looked very nearly respectable. She was most likely the child of a lascar from Bengal or Bombay, as her coffee coloring and fine features suggested, which meant she had probably never known her father. Lascars were still paid only five percent of the wages a British sailor made, and they lived in near slave conditions aboard the ships that hired them for three-year stints. I had read that there were an estimated fifty thousand lascars in Britain, and as long as the captains kept hiring them as strong, hardy, cheap labor, the numbers would continue to grow.

Her parentage, her age, and her status as a workhouse-living, Ragged-School-going street rat gave her exactly the vantage point needed to acquire the understanding of predatory behavior that allowed her to survive this long. Perhaps I shouldn't have been so surprised at the philosophical bend to her thoughts. One could live through broken bones much less painfully than a broken spirit, though it was often surprisingly difficult to have the one without the other.

"Maybe that's the sort of thing I want from you, Jess – that kind of wisdom."

She scoffed again, with an eye-roll for emphasis. "That's just daft. It takes no more than livin' with yer eyes open to see what's in front of yer face."

It was the wisest thing I'd heard all week.

Charlie had spent her day with the other irregulars, teaching them how to do whatever task she had to do, from weeding the garden to putting up the tomatoes she seemed to be able to grow just by smiling at them. One whole wall was planted with them, and her skill at making things flourish seemed to find its voice with the tomatoes *and* the children.

Little Oliver still had tomato sauce from supper in his hair, even after Huff had done him the great service of licking his head, and Jess and Reesy took charge of getting the younger two clean and ready for bed. I sat on the floor of the library with Gryf's head in my lap and watched the lamplight flicker on the spines of the books as I recounted the day with Charlie.

"Of all the things that happened today, the one I feel best about was buying the debt of the seamstress so she could have her sewing machine back," I said. Jess and I had regaled Charlie with the tale of our adventure at the Langham Hotel, and I had spent the last fifteen minutes describing the inside of Mrs. Dorne's pawnshop.

"The whole time I was looking at that treadle machine I was thinking how easy it would be to add a motor to it. The alternating current, three-phase rotating magnetic field motor has already been invented by Tesla and put in use by Galileo Ferraris – it wouldn't take much to build a version of it small enough to power a sewing machine."

Charlie raised an eyebrow. "The power station Ferraris built only serves the street lights. Even Parliament still uses gas lamps."

"Well, I've been thinking …"

Charlie's smile lit her eyes like flickering flames. "Yes?"

I looked around our library, the walls heavy with books, the walls covered in dark green damask velvet to mask the soot stains from the gas flames in the wall sconces. I'd been at war with myself over whether to choose the room for the library with the most windows, ergo, the most natural light, or the fewest, so as not to damage the books with sun-fading.

"What if I powered our house with electricity?"

The raised eyebrow was back. "You know how to wire a house?"

I grinned. "Theoretically. How hard could it be?"

She laughed and leaned down to kiss me. "I would be very cross with you if you electrocuted yourself or burned down the house."

"Well, first I think I'd have to try it someplace else, and since London only has a few coal-burning steam turbine power plants and no proper grid yet ..."

She giggled, and I pretended not to notice that I sounded slightly ridiculous. "I was thinking maybe we could rent a commercial building, and then wire it for electricity. Then perhaps I could fit some sewing machines with small motors for a few of Mrs. Dorne's more industriously inclined clients?"

Charlie had stopped giggling, and I peeked at her face with trepidation.

She was staring at me, and I couldn't tell if it was shock or horror that made her eyes look like pools of the deepest blue on her face.

She stood up and began pacing the room as she spoke. "The women would be working for themselves. We would just provide the working capital, and perhaps a small loan to get started, in exchange for … what? What would make sense?" Animation lit every part of her from within when she returned her gaze to me.

I was making this up as I went along, but it felt right. "There is something I read about in the twenty-first century called a micro-loan. It's a short-term loan with a low interest rate designed to help a small business get on its feet. If, for example, a seamstress were able to work so efficiently that she could make ready-to-wear clothing, or book bags, or backpacks, and if those items were to be sold through, say, the pawnshop? A percentage of the proceeds could pay Mrs. Dorne for the use of her space, a percentage could come back to us to repay the loan, and the rest could go to feed the seamstress's family."

The light in Charlie's eyes had extended to her smile. "And if the seamstress's children were well-fed, they'd be much less likely to pick pockets or need workhouse handouts, and much more likely to be in school to learn a trade."

For the first time since returning to the nineteenth century I felt that I had a reason for being here, a reason to come out of hiding. "We could do this, Charlie. We could actually make a difference."

She bent down and took my face in her hands. "Have I told you lately how extraordinary you are?" She kissed me and then sank down on the floor beside me.

I held her to me as I murmured into her lips. "No, but I definitely think you should."

CHAPTER 15 – LONDON TOWN

Several days later, Wilde, Conan Doyle, and Stoddart made good on their threat to request a guided tour of London from me. I relented on the condition that they surrender to my whims as a tour guide and let me plan the evening. When I told Charlie my intended route, she insisted she help to make it something they'd never forget, and together we hatched our plot.

The men met me outside Parliament, near enough to Stoddart's rented flat in Pimlico that he could walk there without elaborate directions. From there we strolled up to the government buildings which had been constructed on the grounds of what was once Whitehall Palace.

"Gentlemen, I assume you know the history of Whitehall?" I said as we approached the façade to the banqueting house. Conan

Doyle and Wilde did, so I gave a brief history for Stoddart's benefit.

"Originally known as York Place when it was owned by the Archbishop of York in the thirteenth century, it was rebuilt in the fifteenth century, and then expanded so much by Cardinal Wolsey between 1514 and 1528 that it rivaled Lambeth Palace for opulence and greatness. In fact, it was so much grander than even the king's London Westminster residence that in 1529, when Henry VIII removed Wolsey for failing to get the pope to annul his marriage to Catherine of Aragon, Henry decided to acquire York Place for his own. Henry married Anne Boleyn and Jane Seymour at Whitehall Palace, and he built a bowling green, tennis court, a pit for cock-fighting, and a tilting yard for jousting on the grounds. By the time the palace burned to the ground in 1698, it had grown to fifteen hundred rooms – bigger than the Vatican and Versailles at the time."

I pointed up at the elegant structure as we passed it. "The Banqueting House is the only remaining building of the Whitehall Palace complex, but there are other pieces that remain as well. The cock-fighting pit and tennis court survive, for example, and hidden under this—" we stood in front of the government Finance Building, which I knew would one day be rebuilt as the Ministry of Defense, "—is Henry VIII's wine cellar."

The three men listened with avid fascination, and a look of such delight danced across Oscar's face that I couldn't help my own answering grin. The government offices had been closed for several hours. Full dark had fallen, and there were no gaslights in this part of the government complex. With boldness I found intriguing, Conan Doyle tried the door and found it locked. "But how do we get in, man?" he asked urgently.

I brandished a key which Jess had lifted that day. "I know a guy," I said cryptically, using words and a tone lifted straight out of twentieth century gangster movies. Wilde burst out in uproarious laughter, and I raised an eyebrow at him in my best imitation of parental disapproval until he quieted the volume. Finally, I unlocked the door.

"If you'll just follow me please?"

When everyone was inside, I fastened the door behind us so as not to alert cautious night watchmen to our presence, and then led the men to a large storage room on the lower level of the building. In the space behind a shelving unit was a heavy door. I had taken the liberty of picking the old lock earlier, and the door swung open with a groan of weight and age.

The stairs down were old wood, as the door had been, and were cut from thick planks. The darkness into which they stretched was dispelled by strategically placed flickering candles.

"What's this? Are we expected?" Conan Doyle's Scottish burr was more pronounced than usual, perhaps a function of caution, but he stepped forward resolutely and descended the stairs.

Wilde followed directly, and Stoddart hesitated only a moment before he, too, went down the steps. I was last and closed the heavy door behind us.

Charlie waited in the middle of the spectacularly Gothic underground room, with soaring arches held aloft by sturdy columns, and an unbroken brick floor. She had a blanket set out on the floor, and an elaborate picnic supper spread upon it. Oscar gasped and clapped his hands like a schoolboy when he saw her rise to greet them.

"Mrs. Devereux, you astound me!"

"Welcome to King Henry's wine cellar," she said with a beautiful smile.

Introductions were made, glasses of port were poured, and hearty sandwiches were consumed as we all admired the architecture and fine brickwork of the room built by a cardinal and stolen by a king.

Oscar regaled the other men with descriptions of Charlie's extraordinary art, which launched him into a lengthy discussion about Aestheticism in art versus political or social statement pieces. Oscar argued that there is great value in making art purely for the sake of beauty, a sentiment I remembered him expounding upon during our initial meeting the year before. It was an idea he would hold as gospel for the whole of his life, despite the undercurrents of political and social commentary that ran through his writing.

"But what is the point of creating something that has no meaning?" Stoddart argued.

"All art, my dear man, is at once surface and symbol. Those who go beneath the surface do so at their peril. Those who read the symbol do so at their peril. It is the spectator, and not life, that art really mirrors," Oscar said importantly.

Stoddart looked ready to argue when Charlie disarmed him with a smile.

"I draw things as I see them," said my wife with the quiet confidence she had gained during the months she'd spent as the adopted daughter of a sixteenth-century noblewoman, "not as I declare them to be. What is true for me may hold no meaning for you, Mr. Stoddart, or you, Mr. Wilde. I believe we are all a product of our experiences, and as mine have been very different from yours, so too will be the meaning I give to a painting, a story, or a piece of music. Unlike my delightful friend, Oscar, I quite enjoy finding meaning in art, but I recognize it is mine to generate, regardless of the artist's intentions for his or her audience."

Oscar positively beamed at Charlie, and Stoddart seemed to consider her words thoughtfully. "You have given me much to absorb, Mrs. Devereux. I thank you for your insight."

When we had finished our evening's sustenance, we packed up the blanket and baskets and helped Charlie gather the candles. I closed the heavy wooden door of the Whitehall wine cellar softly behind us as Wilde continued his sermon on art in his usual boisterous tones.

"Oscar, if you would be so good as to remain silent until we're out of the building, it would aid us greatly in the avoidance of undue attention," I said quietly. Three sets of startled eyes turned on me when they realized I was serious, and Stoddart appeared about to start sputtering in indignation at the idea that he'd be party to anything which required hiding. I held up a hand for silence. A watchman's light shone in through a window, then continued on down the row of glass until the night outside became dark again.

I finally nodded, and everyone seemed to take a breath before falling into line as we slipped out through the door. I could see the tension in their shoulders, and wondered if I hadn't miscalculated their desire for adventure. I locked the door behind me and pocketed the key, then led Charlie to the side street where a hackney waited. The men remained silent and somewhat tense as Jess stepped out of the small carriage that she'd held for us, and I helped Charlie inside.

"Don't wait up," I said to Charlie as I slipped Jess the key and she seated herself next to my wife.

"Don't let them get you into trouble," she answered, then narrowed her eyes playfully at Oscar. Her tone seemed to lighten something in the mood of the men, and I felt myself relax. "You have the most wonderful voice for oration I've ever heard, Oscar, but you're an abysmal sneak. Take some lessons from my husband on the proper deportment of a thief, at least for tonight," she said.

His look of astonishment made her giggle. "Off you go," I said as I slapped the hackney, and the driver snapped the reins.

I finally turned to face the men and their judgement. "We're not going to steal anything tonight, are we?" Conan Doyle said in low tones that hinted at concern.

I said gravely, "There will be no theft, deliberate or otherwise. I *am* a reformed thief, however, which grants me certain skills of which we will have need on our tour."

The surprise on Oscar's face was replaced by a creeping smile. "You've been telling the truth all along, haven't you? A reformed thief indeed," he snorted. "Well, it's clear that a little breaking and entering never hurt anyone. Come, gentlemen, this game is most definitely afoot."

Conan Doyle's groan was laced with good humor, and Stoddart just looked mildly bewildered as we made our way up the street.

My walking tour of London was less of the "this building was built in 1842 by so and so architect," and more of the "there is a secret door in that attic which affords direct access to the library" variety. I regaled them with my discovery of an old operating theatre in the garret of St. Thomas's Church in Southwark which had been forgotten for nearly thirty years, and a plague pit under St. Bride's Church that was closed up and hidden after a cholera epidemic in 1854. I pulled Stoddart away from a shop window before he could become the victim of an opportunistic pickpocket, and then chased away a gang of street rats who tried to surround him when he stopped to tie his shoe. By the time we arrived at the Grosvenor Gallery, I had shown my companions the entrances to several secret tunnels, and taken them into a hidden garden built on a burial ground. In the garden, I jumped up onto the wall and cat-walked across the top of it, then climbed an apple tree and plucked four ripe apples that I threw down to the men. Then, as we ate our apples, I explained a common getaway path – from the wall, up a tree, across two roofs, and down a series of drainpipes to an access into the Tyburn River tunnel. The shocked expressions on their faces at both my display of acrobatics and my intimate knowledge of the escape routes of criminals might have been entertaining if I had been convinced that the men wouldn't actually call the constables on me. As we continued our tour, however, I was reassured by the speculative look on Oscar's face that led me to believe he had accepted the truth of my past profession and hadn't judged me too harshly for it.

I wasn't sure exactly why I had decided to be so open about my past, except that the months of hiding in my own city had left a sour taste in my mouth. Frankly, I'd been bored, and any young child knew that an instant cure for boredom was the rush of adrenaline that a little danger brought with it.

"As you may know, the Grosvenor Gallery closed down this year, and its walls are now empty of the art that hung here for nearly fifteen years," I said as we arrived at 135 New Bond Street.

"I reviewed the gallery when it first opened, and then again for another show two years later," said Wilde in a subdued yet enthusiastic voice. "It was a remarkable place, and truly dedicated to advancing the ideals of Aestheticism."

The padlock on the side gate was one of those substantial ones intended to look menacing. To me and my lock picks it just meant that the tumblers were bigger and more easily accessed. "Wilde, will you please use your considerable size to shield me from casual view of the street for a few moments? And Stoddart, if you wouldn't mind holding a candle just here?"

The men did as I asked without comment, and Conan Doyle even stepped a little forward to act as lookout. The lock clicked open in less than a minute, and a few seconds later we were inside the yard that stretched behind the gallery.

Massive machines rose up from the cement like the standing stones of a druid ring, casting shadows around the yard that concealed cables and junctions. "Behold, one of London's first private electric power substations," I said quietly.

"A power station at an art gallery? But why?" whispered Stoddart.

"Sir Coutts Lindsey wanted electric lights," said Wilde, looking around him in wonder. "I had no idea this was here, or that it was so very big."

"The power they generated here was enough to sell to neighbors around them," I said as I walked around the massive boilers that stood next to coal hoppers to feed the fires. "It's filthy business though, burning the coal to make steam." Coal dust covered every surface, and with a shudder, I recalled the photos I'd seen in a history book of the thick, pea-soup fog all this coal smoke would cause in the Great Smog of 1952.

"Technology generally is," said Wilde. *Not if I can help it*, I thought as I considered the huge machines. Stoddart and Conan Doyle were happily examining the giant dynamo generators in the yard, exclaiming in delight over the ingenuity of the system. As impressive as it was, I knew I could do better than this, and I wouldn't be using steam to generate the power for my house.

"Psst! Ringo," Wilde whispered to me as he opened a door at the back of the gallery that he had found unlocked. I grinned at his brazen entry, and then followed him in.

The interior of the gallery was empty of course. The air was cold, and the gilt, silk-covered walls were bare of paintings, while the ceiling above was glass with iron bracework that looked like the skeleton of a great beast. Wilde contemplated the silk walls sadly. "So many Aesthetes exhibited here – Whistler ... Frederick Leighton ... did you know that nearly a quarter of the artists on

128

display here were women? Can you imagine the Royal Academy of Arts being so avant garde?" Wilde scoffed quietly. "The public can forgive everything but genius, and in this place the genius abounded unforgivably."

He wandered around the room a few more paces, and then his gaze held a spot on one wall. "Leighton's *Pavonia* spoke the sort of magic that wends its way into men's souls. Her eyes wove tales of bright laughter and deep loves, and one could hear the whispers of secrets from lips that never moved. *Pavonia* is a painting worthy of the meaning your lovely wife insists we all ascribe to the art that moves us. And yet Leighton himself—" Wilde made a dismissive gesture. "The only artists I have known who are personally delightful are bad artists. Good artists exist simply in what they make, and consequently are perfectly uninteresting in what they are."

"I've seen some of Leighton's work, but not *Pavonia*. You make it sound extraordinary." I'd gone to a gallery show of Victorian artists with Charlie in the twenty-first century, just before we were married. She had admired Leighton's work greatly, and although I didn't lay any claim to understanding art, I knew that his paintings had impressed me.

Oscar turned to me and seemed to come back to himself. His eyes narrowed and an eyebrow arched up suggestively, making me wonder if he had somehow known that my own memories had been of a future time. "I happen to know that Leighton is in

France at some conference or other. I would like to show you his *Pavonia*. If I take you to his house, would you help us get in?"

I scowled at him. "He certainly has staff at his house, and I have no interest in becoming overly friendly with Scotland Yard."

He waved his hand. "He has a butler and a maid, and they live on the bottom floor, far from the studio. Come, all this talk of art and secrecy this evening has made me hungry for both, and a painting one must view in secret fits the bill perfectly."

"Charlie told you not to get me into trouble," I said sternly.

"It has become clear to me that you, my dear young man, are entirely capable of getting yourself both into and out of your own trouble. For one who lived such a colorful early life, your choice to hide in your lovely Grayson House is an interesting one. It is safe, yes, but I believe you are a man for whom safety is a straitjacket that binds your mind as well as your limbs."

He gestured outside to the electrical generating plant. "I can see the blueprints for technology beginning to ink themselves in your brain. Now it's time to light the fuse on your imagination with art you've risked something to experience."

I sighed, but there was a smile hiding in it when I answered him. "Your power to compel is very nearly dangerous in its effectiveness." I studied him with a critical eye. Oscar had worn a dark velvet coat for our night out, which would serve our purposes perfectly. I, on the other hand, would likely need a fist full of coal dust to accomplish the task at hand. My wife had begun a collection of all the things she found in my pockets, but I doubted she would be amused by the coal dust she'd find tomorrow if I didn't remember to dump it before I got home.

I held the door for Wilde to exit the gallery. "I think we should bid goodnight to the two very upright gentlemen with us, as I don't feel their morality can bend beyond empty government buildings and abandoned galleries." I picked up a handful of coal dust from the yard with a smirk of amusement. "You, however, have the morals of a cat on the trail of a very tasty mouse."

Chapter 16 - Leighton House

We saw Conan Doyle and Stoddart into a hackney with promises to reveal more secrets of London another time, and then set off at a brisk walking pace in the direction of Kensington.

Along the way, Wilde regaled me with what he knew of Sir Frederic Leighton – fluent in French, German, and Italian from a youth spent on the Continent with his family, he studied art in Italy, and his wealth came both from his family and his own labors.

"I heard that one of his paintings sold recently for six thousand," said Oscar in a droll tone. "Considering his house cost something close to five, I'd say he's doing well for himself."

"You sound as though you don't care for the man," I observed dryly.

"I admire his work with the whole of my being, but as I said before, he is impossible to truly know, as he leaves nothing of himself off the canvas."

The walk from Grosvenor Hill to Holland Park took nearly an hour, but it was quite delightful to stroll through Hyde Park on a crisp night with few pedestrians. Oscar asked questions about my days as a thief, and I told him that I'd been nicknamed Keys because I could open any door by climbing through a window.

"Where did the name Ringo come from?" he asked.

"Saira called me that, and it stuck."

"And Devereux? I believe that was the last name of Saira's husband, Archer?" Oscar was fishing, and I'd allow him small bites to keep the larger questions at bay.

"Archer Devereux is the younger son of a duke who believes Archer is dead. When Charlie and I married, one of Archer's wedding presents to us was his name, which he registered to a bank account at Rothschild's. It's as close a thing to a birth certificate as I have ever had, and Archer is my brother in all but blood, so it, too, stuck."

And that was all I would say about that.

The houses of much of Holland Park were solidly middle class, and many had been built within the previous fifty years in classic Victorian style. Holland Park Circle, which we approached from Kensington High Street, was an enclave of successful artists; Leighton's house at 2 Holland Park Road was among the largest.

133

The house, constructed of red brick and vaguely Moorish in design, occupied a large lot that backed up to the park itself. It was past midnight and the street was deserted, but I crept down the side of the house to the open land behind it in order to draw as little attention as possible. Oscar followed my lead.

I tucked myself back against the trunk of a tree and bid Oscar to do the same. Then I rubbed coal dust on my hands and face to dim the brightness of my skin. A small part of me wished I'd brought Jess with me tonight, as it would have been good to have a skilled partner in crime, but she hadn't shown any inclination toward thieving since we took her in, and this adventure definitely fell into the category of breaking and entering.

I wondered what the excuse to the police officer might sound like if we were caught. *Sorry, sir. We just wanted to see a painting.* I shook my head, unable even to imagine it.

The doors on the ground floor would all be locked from the inside, most likely with bolts, as the house was too prominent and the appearance of wealth too obvious for the staff not to secure the entrances while Leighton was away. I sighted a second floor window with a deep ledge that looked promising, and with a quick hand signal to Oscar to wait for me, I stole across the lawn to the house and began scaling the bricks.

I'd worn boots in anticipation of a night of walking, but the grooves between the bricks were not deep enough for thick soles, so I slipped off my shoes and socks and left them by the back door. It had been some time since I'd scaled anything in bare feet, and it proved quite a different experience when one had a full-grown man's body rather than a wiry adolescent's. I was stronger, which helped, but I was also heavier, and the extra bulk made the climb trickier than it had ever been before.

As I'd hoped, the upper floor window was unlocked, which meant it was likely a bedroom. I sincerely hoped Oscar's information was good, and that except for two servants, the house would be empty. The window slid easily, and a moment later I was inside the dark room, closing the window softly behind me and sending a silent prayer of relief to Hermes, god of thieves, that I'd made it.

The sound of a ticking clock was the only one I heard until something warm wound its way around my legs. Then all I could hear was my heart slamming in my chest until I realized it was just a cat rubbing its fur on my trousers. I reached down to scratch it for a moment while I calmed the panicky feeling that had shaken me. I had never been one to panic, and in that moment I was glad I'd agreed to this madness. If a cat could send my heart racing after just a few years away from the trade, perhaps it was a good idea to get back into practice.

With new determination, I gave the cat a final scratch on the head as my eyes adjusted to the darkness in the house, and then I made my way through the sparely-furnished room and down the hall to the staircase.

135

I was very glad for my bare feet upon my descent to the first floor, for the stairs ended in a two-story, Arabesque hall covered in tiles and woodwork from Damascus. The predominant color was blue, but every color of the rainbow could be found in the intricate artistry of the hand-painted tiles. In the center of the hall was a fountain, from which water bubbled softly, but even such a delightfully mild sound filled the room with its echo. It was quite possibly the most beautiful room I'd ever seen, and yet from a thief's perspective, it was also the most dangerous.

I moved noiselessly to the back of the house and slid the bolt on the servants' entrance. Oscar was there a moment later, and I indicated silently that he should leave his shoes at the door.

Once through the Arabesque hall, Oscar took over as tour guide. He led the way to a large, open studio on the east side of the house. Big windows lined one wall, but heavy drapes were closed over them, presumably because Leighton was away. I pulled a candle stub from my pocket and lit it with a match.

The breath rushed out of me as the candlelight illuminated scores of paintings hanging on the walls and propped against them on the floor. There were portraits and landscapes, sunsets and nudes, battle scenes, and quiet moments of tenderness, all rendered in vivid colors and the precise strokes of a confident brush. I lit another candle stub and gave it to Oscar so he could go off in search of his *Pavonia*, and I could explore the studio on my own.

The paintings held magic within them, and the kind of breathtaking beauty to which it was impossible to do justice with words. There were pencil and chalk studies tacked next to some of the completed paintings, and many of the works seemed to be of the same young blonde woman. I thought about what Oscar had said – that the great artists leave all of themselves on their canvases. What I felt from the portraits of the women was not the artist's adoration or attraction, but his care and protection, as though they were fragile things he was meant to keep safe.

My path was aimless as I wandered around the studio, and it gravitated to whichever image caught my imagination next. I wished Charlie were beside me, so I could see it through her eyes and experience the paintings the way she saw light, and shadow, and color. One particular study caught my eye. This woman was depicted differently than the blonde, and the story Leighton told about her felt less protective, and more … fascinated. The woman lay curled in sleep, with oleander flowers over her head in all their poisonous beauty. Her dress was long and flowing, and it hugged the curves of her figure in a way that was both innocent and suggestive. One bare foot peeked out from under the filmy cloth, and her long, curly hair lay draped above her.

The study was in pencil and chalk, but I knew the finished painting as *Flaming June*, which had been on loan to the gallery where I'd seen Leighton's paintings. In the finished painting, the woman's dress would be a bright and beautiful sunset orange, and her hair would be a striking true red. This study provoked me. It whispered of secrets and mysteries, and of attraction that went far beyond the physical. If my sense of propriety and responsibility had been less well-developed, I might have given in to my instinct to roll that pencil drawing up and put it in my pocket. I was also quite aware of the irony that I – breaker-and-enterer of the guiltiest variety – was having pangs of conscience.

As I moved away from that compelling image, my bare foot felt a seam in the wood and I knelt to examine it. My candlelight showed a well-fitted trap door set into the studio floor, and a moment later I found the catch to open it. The space it concealed was not deep, but it was large enough to hold a stack of several stretched canvases ready to be painted. A clever storage place in a room built specifically for an artist – I admired the practicality of Leighton, who seemed so utterly focused on creativity, and I thought I might one day seek an introduction to the man himself.

The trap door creaked as I lowered it to the floor, and my self-preservation instinct returned at full volume. It was time for us to leave this remarkable place. I went in search of Oscar and found him in a large, silk-hung hall at the back of the house. He stared at a painting of a dark-haired young woman which hung upon one wall.

"It's spectacular, isn't it?" Oscar whispered when he sensed my presence behind him.

I studied the painting. The dark haired beauty in the portrait was certainly breathtaking, but I wondered if Oscar's attraction to the painting was made of something more complex than feminine beauty.

"We need to go," I breathed, finally tearing my eyes from the splendor that surrounded us. Oscar nodded his agreement and led the way back to the door I'd opened for him. He pulled his shoes back on while I tied a small string in a loose slipknot around the bolt. As I closed the door behind us, I used the string to pull the bolt home before tugging the string free and through the crack in the door. I stuffed the string into one boot as I pulled it on, then carefully emptied the charcoal from my pockets as we hurried away from the house.

It wasn't until we'd walked for several blocks that Oscar finally spoke.

"The *Pavonia* was as beautiful as I'd remembered her," he said.

"Were you worried?" I asked.

He looked at me for a long moment before turning his gaze back to the street in front of us. "The longer I live, the more cynical I become. I was afraid I had lost the ability to see beauty so purely and completely, and I feared my view would be tainted by my weariness with the complaints and concerns that reduce ideals to pettiness." He sighed in a way that spoke of quiet sadness rather than drama. "I am a dreamer, Ringo. For a dreamer is one who can only find his way by moonlight, and his punishment is that he sees the dawn before the rest of the world."

The eastern sky was just beginning to show the first signs of orange, and it brought to mind the painting of *Flaming June* I would one day see in its glorious, finished state.

"There is something that can be said for dawn," I said.

He smiled sadly. "What wisdom do you share with me at the end of an adventure such as we've had this night?"

I smiled. "Dawn is the moment between night and day, when color wipes the darkness away and anything feels possible." I gripped his shoulder. "It's a new day, Oscar, and starting a new day with a friend like you speaks to its worthiness."

Chapter 17 – The Man with Red Hair

A week later, I was on my way home from the university library when Jess stepped out in front of me. I had been holed up in the library for days looking for every bit of information I could find about electro-magnetic engines, and I hadn't seen her other than at meals. I hadn't expected her and would have jumped out of my skin if my street skills hadn't been sharpened recently.

"Are you trying to startle me, or did your cloak of invisibility slip off?"

She scowled at me. "Cloak of—?"

"—Nevermind," I said quickly. It was my own fault she'd startled me. My arms weren't full of books this time, but engines and generators filled my brain and dulled my eyes to shadows that held too still.

"Lucy's mum wants ye," she said in a tone that told me it was a summons, not a request.

"Right. Lead on, MacDuff."

She looked at me strangely as we started to walk to Mrs. Dorne's shop. "That's from *King Solomon's Mines*."

I was shocked that she knew this, or any literary reference for that matter. "That's right. But it's actually misquoted from Shakespeare. It should be 'Lay on, MacDuff,' which means 'give it your best fight.' How do you know *King Solomon's Mines*?"

She shrugged. "It's a game we play in the park sometimes. We're in deepest Africa, and Reesy always tries to be Allan Quatermain, but I always win."

She didn't answer my question, and based on the sly smile she wore, she knew it perturbed me. Obscure information was my stock in trade, and I couldn't tell if it delighted or annoyed me that Jess seemed to share the same stock.

The pawnshop wore sunset-colored light reflected on its window when we arrived, and the three gold balls hung like glittering jewels above it. Jess pushed open the door and slid inside. She blended instantly among the bric-a-brac and was nearly invisible in the dimly lit shop, which was lit by gas light, I noted, as was nearly every other shop on Paddington Street. The street lights had been converted to electricity through most of Marylebone, though there were still lamplighters to be seen in some of the less affluent residential areas.

My musings about electricity were cut short when I caught sight of an extraordinarily red-haired man who sat in a dainty Queen Anne chair near the counter where Mrs. Dorne stood watchfully.

"This is the man I told ye about, Mr. Wilson," she said to the man, who must have been in his forties, though his hair was untouched by gray. It really was the most exceptional color of red, and matched perfectly the bushy red mustache that so dominated his upper lip it blocked all opportunity to lip-read his response – which was a necessity, given the man's mumbled words.

I held my hand out to shake his, and it seemed to startle him, because he nearly knocked over the chair in his haste to stand. "My name is Devereux. Good to meet you, Mr. Wilson."

His grip was firm and his fingers were calloused. "Good to meet you too, Mr. Devereux," he mumbled.

The man's eyes were red-rimmed and dull with fatigue, and he looked as though he carried the weight of the world on his shoulders. Mrs. Dorne stepped forward from behind the counter and directed her words to me. "Mr. Wilson is my landlord. This were once the least of 'is three pawnbroker shops, and 'e let the business to me to focus 'is attentions on the other two. 'E 'ad to close the Westminster shop, and now the Leadenhall shop's near done for too. Mr. Wilson just informed me 'e 'as to sell this shop out from under me. I'm 'opin', Mr. Devereux, that you'd be willin' to 'elp."

To help with what? Her purchase of the pawnshop, or something else? I studied Mr. Wilson carefully before I finally spoke. "Might I inquire, Mr. Wilson, as to why you have recently taken up such studious writing?"

I was rewarded with a wide-eyed start from him, and the barest hint of a smirk from her. So, she was enjoying this, was she? Jess nudged forward so she could hear Wilson's response.

"How ... how could you possibly know such a thing, young man?"

Young man, was it? Fine, then, he got both barrels. "Your cuffs are stained and your elbows are shiny from resting on a wooden tabletop. Your grip is firmer in your right hand than your left, and much firmer than the paleness of your hands, rather than the tan hands of outdoor work, would indicate. The callouses on the first and middle finger of your right hand are new and big enough to indicate many recent hours of writing by hand. You've been working in low light, as your reddened eyes and newly acquired squint would indicate, and your stooped posture tells me the chair was uncomfortable and the table too low."

He stared at me for a long moment, as though processing everything I'd just said. "Oh, well, right then. That seems simple enough," he finally mumbled. I barely contained the smile that threatened when reluctance tinged others' acceptance of my deductions.

"Like Mrs. Dorne said," Mr. Wilson continued, "my shops have been having a spot of trouble."

The shops weren't having trouble. Shops don't have trouble. People have trouble turning a profit or managing a business. An observant person might have discerned my thoughts in the polite expression of disinterest I likely wore.

Mr. Wilson was not an observant person, and he launched directly into his tale. "Now, I'm a *Telegraph* man, always have been. None of that fancy *Daily Mail* business for me. I like my news plain and simple, and I spend a penny a week to have it delivered right to my doorstep. Now one day, round about six weeks ago, I open the *Telegraph* to the advertisements, just as always, and what do I see? An advert, right there, calling all redheaded men to come to an office in Shrewsbury for the chance to earn a good salary for simple work. It was very particular about what color red a man's hair had to be, and men with orange or auburn hair need not apply."

"The Redheaded Men's Club?" I asked with some alarm before I could stop myself. I had a horrible feeling I knew where this was going.

"That's what I said, didn't I? Well, I took myself right down to that office on the appointed day, and wouldn't you know it, there were twenty or thirty men, with all manner of red hair, waiting in line for their chance at the job. It took nearly an hour to finally be seen, and wasn't there a line behind me twice as long when I finally filled out my paperwork."

The sense of déjà vu was nearly overwhelming, though I had the niggling thought that this was going to be more than just the source for a Conan Doyle story. "What sort of information did the paperwork ask for?" I said.

"Only my name, occupation, and place of business," he responded. "The secretary said it was all that was necessary because the real qualification was the color of my hair. And in fact, when she returned with my paperwork, she said that the Board of Directors of the Redheaded Men's Club had seen me from the window and had determined I was perfect for the job. I was given an address in Clerkenwell and told to be there every day from ten in the morning until five in the evening, and for my trouble I would be paid four pounds sterling per week."

He looked utterly forlorn, and I had to struggle to hear him murmur through the great mustache again. "The loss of that princely sum is the most painful bit of all."

"What happened the first day you arrived at the Clerkenwell address?"

"The secretary met me there, unlocked an office, and gave me an *Encyclopaedia Britannica*, a pen, and a notebook. She told me that the Board of Directors was most interested in my dedication to a task and the perfection with which I completed it, so would I please copy out the encyclopedia beginning with the subjects in the letter A." Mr. Wilson flexed his hand as if in memory of a painful task. "Then she left and said she would return for me at five o'clock, and that I was not to leave the office for any reason lest they deem me unfit to receive my pay at the end of the week. And let me tell you, I made a far sight more money in the six weeks I copied out the encyclopedia than in six months in the pawnshop."

"Just six weeks?" I asked.

I braced myself for the forlorn mumble. "I arrived at the office last week to find the door locked and no sign of the secretary. At first I was relieved. I hadn't even gotten to the Bs, and I now know far more about aardvarks and antelopes than I had ever hoped to. I reopened my pawnshop and rested my hand, but after one week without the income from the Redheaded Men's Club, I am without the means to continue holding this property."

I cocked an eyebrow at him. "Putting aside the issue of your blackmailer for the moment, tell me about the members of the Redheaded Men's Club."

Mr. Wilson's expression of horror would have been amusing if I hadn't expected it. Jess giggled quietly from her hiding spot, and Mrs. Dorne murmured something under her breath that sounded vaguely like a curse.

Before he could sputter a denial, I interrupted. "Mr. Wilson, you don't have the look of a drinker, nor the temperament of a

147

womanizer. You were once a successful businessman, to which your three pawnshops would attest, yet now you suffer at the loss of four pounds a week. You've either gambled away your money and now owe a moneylender, which seems unlikely in the face of your relative lack of fear, or you've done something unethical or criminal – not really my first assumption about you, but possible nonetheless – and someone has caught you at it. It's the catching that's the important bit of it, really." Mrs. Dorne had carefully schooled her expression, but I did think she rather enjoyed my dissection of the man who threatened her livelihood.

I studied Mr. Wilson's countenance, which paled when I said, "While I don't particularly care to know the details, I do think the blackmailer will factor into your story."

He could only gape at me as I continued. "Of more interest to me at the moment though, is whatever you can remember about the Redheaded Men's Club."

Then Mr. Wilson actually sputtered. Little flecks of spittle hung from his mustache like ornaments from a tree. "But there was no one. I never saw another redheaded man at all."

"Describe the secretary then, if you please."

"Well, she was redheaded too, obviously." Mr. Wilson was barely recovered from his sputtering incident, and had not yet cleared his mustache of its ornamentation. Thankfully, Mrs. Dorne produced a handkerchief and handed it to the man, who absently dabbed at his face and accidentally wiped away the offending droplets.

"Obviously." I didn't bother to point out the *men's club* portion of their title. "And was she young, old, tall, short, slender, rotund?"

"Yes."

Mrs. Dorne snorted in annoyance, and I gritted my teeth. "Which one, Mr. Wilson?"

He shook himself and finally focused on my face again. "I ... I'm not entirely sure."

I took a deep, bracing breath. "How old would you say she was?"

Mr. Wilson's gaze cast about frantically. "Not as old as her," he pointed at Mrs. Dorne, "or as young as ... as that." This time his finger wavered as he pointed at Jess, who bared her teeth at him. He looked away quickly, and I caught her satisfied smirk.

His description so far was spectacularly unhelpful, and my patience was rapidly diminishing. "Her figure and her height, then?"

"She was ... medium."

"Medium." I might have actually hated the man with that one word. "What is medium, Mr. Wilson? Describe it."

"In the middle, middling, average, unremarkable – just medium."

I was convinced that the only things remarkable about Mr. Wilson were the color of his hair and the quantity of his synonyms. I found myself itching to escape the confines of the pawnshop and the narrowness of the person before me.

"Right, then. Mr. Wilson, you will give the address of your shop to Mrs. Dorne, and when I visit you there tomorrow morning, you will provide me with the details of your blackmailer."

He opened his mouth to protest, so I pulled out the menacing voice and used its amplification and depth to end the conversation entirely. "Good day, Mr. Wilson."

It worked, and I heard nothing further from him as I stalked out of the pawnshop. I couldn't speak for several blocks until my annoyance faded. Then I began to laugh.

Jess had trailed me in silence until then, and she finally approached me warily. "'Ave ye gone a little mad?"

"Probably." I wiped my eyes and caught my breath. The laughter had cleared away the tight-chested frustration that my conversation with Mr. Wilson had inspired, and I felt like myself again. "What do you make of Mr. Wilson's problem?" I asked her as we continued walking.

"Somebody wanted 'im out of the way."

"Exactly. It does suggest a rather elaborate scheme though – going so far as to place an advertisement in the one newspaper he reads. I wouldn't be surprised if the blackmail was set up beforehand simply to make him desperate enough to take such a mindless job."

"Seems like a lot of trouble to get into a pawnshop," Jess said skeptically.

"It certainly does."

It also seemed likely that whatever crime had been plotted had already been committed. Why else allow the dimwitted pawnbroker back into his shop?

We took a familiar path through Regent's Park as we reviewed the particulars of our encounter with Mr. Wilson. A child ran by holding a pinwheel high above her head. She laughed as the wind spun the brightly colored paper, and I caught a glimpse of a childhood neither Jess nor I ever had. The spinning paper wheel was still on my mind as we crossed the footbridge over the river, and inspiration completely unrelated to our conversation suddenly struck me. I stopped and turned back to stand in the middle of the bridge.

Jess looked at me in confusion as I gazed down at the Tyburn River that ran beneath us.

"Yes," I whispered, as all thoughts of the redheaded man deserted me.

"What?" Jess joined me on the bridge and tried to understand what I saw.

My eyes met hers, and I was suddenly giddy.

"I know how I'm going to power our house."

Chapter 18 - The Tyburn

The Tyburn River gave its name to the area of Tyburn, an original manor of Marylebone, which was recorded in the Domesday Book of 1086. The river began in Hampstead, at Shepard's Well, which was alleged to be crystal clear drinking water. By the time it wound its way along Scholars' Pond Sewer through South Hampstead and then became a proper aboveground river in Regent's Park, however, it developed an unmistakable pungency. From its aboveground presence in the park, it dropped down a tunnel and into a culvert on a stealthy course that took it beneath the garden of Grayson House. It then continued south, under St. James's Park, until finally trickling to an ignoble end in the Thames River at Pimlico.

Jess and I entered the Tyburn River tunnel in Regent's Park just after sunset with the intention of finding the right power-generating circumstances at a location into which I could wire electricity. Ideally the place would have a back garden for a generator, with enough water volume running beneath it to install a small hydro-electric turbine. I wore tall boots, and Charlie had loaned Jess a pair of hers with extra socks to fill the gaps. The boots would probably have to be thrown away after the excursion, but at least our feet were protected from the objectionable and repulsive things that no doubt lurked under the water.

We each carried a lantern and a tall stick, and I had tucked extra candles into my pockets in case the oil ran low. I hoped we wouldn't be underground for long, because I didn't care to think about losing my way in the pitch black tunnels that twisted and turned under London.

There was a river grate in the corner of our walled garden that allowed for ventilation of the underground river channels. I had dropped a long rope down and tied it off so I could locate our house from beneath. Jess and I began at the park and followed the river into the tunnel as it wound a predictable path toward that grate. Within a hundred yards I'd found the rope.

I tied my lantern to it so the light dangled above my head and illuminated that portion of the river tunnel. It was about ten feet wide, and according to the depth notches on my stick, the water was about three feet deep. It moved at a fair pace through the tunnel, though I thought I could make it move faster.

It also hadn't picked up a lot of the sewage I knew would pour into it later down the line, so the stench was more of the

organic, animal variety than that of human origin. I used my stick
to take measurements, then untied the lantern and continued
down the tunnel along the brick ledge that acted as a walkway.

"Have you ever spent the night underground?" I whispered
to Jess.

"Once," she said with a shudder. "And I won't do it again if I
can 'elp it. I go a bit mad in the dark if I'm there too long."

"I knew a bloke once, a long time ago. He was twelve, and he
spent a month hiding in a priest hole. He came out a bit off his
head, and I'm not sure he ever truly recovered from it. I've never
been able to find out what happened to him in the end." Mostly
because 'a long time ago' meant three hundred years, and the
records that survived from Tudor England didn't include the fate
of the younger brothers of traitors who had to hide their identities
to survive.

"Why did 'e 'ave to 'ide for a month?"

"His brother had plotted against the queen, so they hunted
the whole family." I didn't bother to explain that the queen in
question was not Victoria, but Mary Tudor, though I doubted the
discrepancy would be noted.

Jess was silent a long time, and the only sound was the clap of
our boots along the old bricks. "Ye know things ye shouldn't,"
she finally said solemnly.

"Probably." I tried not to let my surprise show, but the girl
was remarkably astute.

154

"Why?"

"Because I've been places, and seen things. And because I'm always reading, and asking questions, and looking for answers."

She grunted unhappily. "Ye're tellin' me nothin' I can sink my teeth into."

"What answers would you like to hear?" My silence on nearly everything was an ingrained habit, born of a need to hide what I knew about the past and the future.

"Ye mean to bring electric lights to yer 'ouse, yet ye shouldn't know 'ow to do a thing like that when no one else does. Ye say ye grew up a thief on the street, and ye live in a fine 'ouse, with a library bigger than any I've ever seen, full of books ye've read. And ye're barely a man grown, yet old men listen to ye despite themselves. Ye've taken us in, and I catch ye lookin' at us like you're not sure why we're there. I catch ye lookin' at yer missus that way too sometimes, like ye can't quite understand how she came to be married to ye. And to top all that off, I can't understand why I just said all those things to ye when we're underground and ye could just walk off with the light and leave me 'ere to find my way out." She scoffed at herself and then went silent beside me.

We followed a sharp bend in the tunnel, and it suddenly narrowed dangerously. The ledge where we walked was still wide enough to follow in single file, but I worried we'd soon find ourselves with no easy path.

"Do you have friends, Jess?" I finally asked.

"Ye know I do. They're all asleep in beds in yer 'ouse."

"How well do they know you?"

"Same as I know meself," she said confidently. "We've 'ad the same life, more or less, and the same stories."

"What about people who don't have your stories? Do you think you could ever share as much of yourself with them as you do with your friends?" I asked quietly.

Jess didn't hesitate. "They wouldn't understand."

"That's how it is with me. I have stories most people wouldn't understand, and the friends that do know me live very far away. Charlie knows me, and maybe what you see when I look at her is that I can't believe how lucky I am that she loves me anyway."

She was quiet a long time after that. The rats skittered around corners ahead of us, and the tunnel made another sharp turn. It narrowed again on the straightaway, and I stuck my stick into the water. It was nearly six feet deep and the force of the current nearly pulled the stick out of my hand. This was the spot.

I held the lantern up high to look for landmarks. I had a general sense of the river's path under the city, but it seemed simpler to work backwards from river access to physical address. This was why I moved forward along the ledge carefully, searching for any sign of an opening to the street above. Ahead of us was another grate, and a small ladder of metal rungs set into the bricks rose up from the ledge. I handed Jess my lantern and began to climb.

The rungs were firmly set into the brickwork, and I realized the Tyburn had likely only been bricked over here in the past fifty years. I reached the top in a matter of seconds, held onto the grate with one hand and pushed with the other. The metal didn't move, so I peered through the grate from every angle. There was no sound of horse hooves or wheels, or even people talking above the grate. When my face was positioned in the far left corner, though, I could see the cornice at the top of a building. The moon was only just bright enough to illuminate dental moulding and a rosette. I hoped it was enough to find from the street.

Just then a dog barked above me, and a cold, wet nose sniffed my fingers as they gripped the metal. I almost lost my footing in my surprise as I jerked my hand back, but at the whimper above me, I looked up. A floppy-eared beagle looked down at me with a mournful gaze.

"Hi, pup," I whispered to it.

He whined again and then pawed at the grate.

"It's late for you to be outside, isn't it?" I said quietly. I put my open hand against the grate and the beagle sniffed my palm before trying unsuccessfully to lick it.

"I'll bring you a treat when I come to find you, alright?" I said, as I backed down the ladder.

The dog whined again and stood watching me until I was down on the ledge.

Jess still held the lantern, and in the light that bathed the tunnel, the beagle at the grate was invisible above us. "Can ye find yer way there from the street?" she asked, as we started back the way we came.

"Maybe. I need to borrow one of Gryf's bones first, though."

It only took about an hour of searching before we found the right building in the section of Marylebone I'd marked as the likely location for that second, accessible grate. Then it was just a matter of finding a building with a back garden that housed a beagle that I hoped hadn't been put away for the night.

And in fact, his owners were properly negligent, because the poor dog was still outside and was lying on top of the grate as if waiting for me to return. I hopped over the wall, and he came careening across the dirt yard to bump into my legs with happy whimpers of greeting.

Jess crouched on top of the wall and watched me wrestle with the beagle for a few minutes before I gave him a final scratch and handed him the bone. She surveyed the yard skeptically.

"It's full of junk," she whispered in disgusted fascination.

We'd come down the back alley, so I wasn't sure if the building was residential or commercial, but I knew I wanted it. The garden, full of bits of metal and scraps of building materials

158

though it was, would be perfect for housing a small electrical generator, powered by the force of the culverted Tyburn River.

"Let's go see what we're up against," I whispered back.

I jumped up onto the back wall, and we slipped down the alley to the nearest cross street, then back out to Baker Street. I counted five buildings down, and then looked up to double check the dental moulding and corner rosettes. It appeared to be a duplex, with unit A on the ground floor, and unit B upstairs. If I meant to electrify one floor, I'd have to do them both, so I made note of the house number and resolved to send an estate agent around to the owner with an offer.

It wasn't until later, after a long bath, as I lay in our bed recounting the adventure in the Tyburn tunnel, that I groaned out loud at the remarkable coincidence I'd just realized.

"What is it?" Charlie asked, her eyes meeting mine with concern.

"The address of the building I want us to buy."

"Yes?" she asked.

I shuddered to think of my next luncheon with Conan Doyle. "It's 221 Baker Street."

Charlie's laughter resulted in a fit of the hiccups, about which I was profoundly unsympathetic.

Chapter 19 – Barings Bank

Leadenhall Market had been rebuilt with iron and glass just nine years before, replacing the stone market that had been built after the Great London Fire of 1666. The place had been a poultry and cheese market since the early 1400s, and in my misguided youth, was always a favorite place to filch a sausage roll and drink the dregs of the drunkards' ale cups.

I sat at a table in the corner of a cheesemonger's stall, sipping heavily-sugared coffee and taking huge bites of a truly excellent goat-cheese-topped slice of bread. Jess slipped up next to me, wearing her delivery boy's clothes and cap and nibbling on a meat pasty.

We were early. The pawnbroker's shop was a block away, but still closed for business, and I suffered from an acute desire to spend as little time with the mumbling red-haired man as possible. I had been up since well before dawn, sketching ideas for my plans to electrify the Baker Street property. As the tunnel under our garden was wider than the one under 221 Baker Street, the water moved at a slower pace and would require greater volume to turn the turbines I was planning to build. Baker Street would be a less challenging project on which to test my designs, and would ultimately, I hoped, house the motorized sewing machines and other gadgets of industry I might one day find the courage to invent for the working people of Marylebone.

I was still drawing when Jess finally spoke the words she'd seemed to be holding all morning.

"I'll tell ye my story, if ye like."

I looked up in surprise. She'd been closed up tight since she came down to the kitchen at daybreak, and I never imagined *that* had been on her mind.

I put my pen down and waited in silence. I'd schooled my expression to polite interest, figuring she'd say whatever she'd say in her own time.

"I'll wait 'til we're walkin' a fair distance though, if ye don't mind, so I don't 'ave to see yer face when I do."

I took a sip of coffee, wincing at the bitterness of overbrewed sludge that no amount of sugar could erase. "I'd be honored to know your story whenever you share it."

She nodded once, quickly, as the clock struck the hour. The notebook with my generator designs went into a pocket, and I stood to go. "After you," I said casually. She led the way out of the market and across Leadenhall Street.

Wilson's pawnshop was less than a minute away, down a short, narrow passage, and it occupied the lower level of a two-story structure. Gracechurch Street and Bishopsgate were wide boulevards lined with churches and big banks on either side, but the smaller offshoot streets like Leadenhall were stacked two and three deep with commercial buildings and small shops like this one, and filled with people just trying to make a living.

The shop was still closed, despite the late morning hour, and I sighed in frustration. As we stood in front of the dirty windows filled with a jumble of random items, I spotted a broken fence rail leaning against the side of the house. "Get me that bit of wood, will you?" I asked Jess. I'd begun stomping my feet on the pavement just outside the walls.

Jess brought me the fence rail, and I used it to tap the sidewalk. She looked at me oddly for the space of about three seconds before she understood what I was doing, and then she joined me in my strange, primitive dance outside of the pawnshop.

Finally, I was satisfied, and I stopped and looked up at the buildings which surrounded the pawnshop. I turned back down the alley and stalked around the corner onto Bishopsgate, counting buildings as I walked. Jess scampered in front of me and then stopped at number six. She stared up at the words carved in bold letters into the stone facing.

"Ba … bar …"

I didn't sound it out for her. At her insistence, we'd been working on her letters every night until she couldn't hold her eyes open anymore.

"Bar … ings. Barings Ba … Barings Bank," she finally said proudly, with a look at me for confirmation.

"Indeed. Barings is second-oldest merchant bank in the world, and the actual party from whom the Americans purchased the Louisiana Territory in 1802, despite the fact that Britain and France were at war, and the sale had the effect of financing Napoleon's war effort."

"Why'd they do that?" Jess asked with a critical stare at the venerable stone building that loomed above us.

"They, and the British politicians who backed them, wagered that the expansion would result in the familiar American pattern of the extermination of native populations, the importation of African slaves, and the production and export of cotton for British mills. In other words, what was essentially treason was also good for the British economy."

My study of the façade had become more of a glare. "I think it may be time to call in Scotland Yard." Even the thought of it gave me chills.

"Why do ye look like ye just ate somethin' sour?" Jess asked.

I sighed and looked her in the eyes. "I admit, I'm less than confident about involving the police. I've never been the one who called them – they were generally called on me."

Jess looked up at me sharply. "Ye're a right proper man with the bearin' to know what ye're about. There's no copper in London who'll think yer other than an upper class toff to be listened to and respected."

The vehemence of her words startled me, and I glanced at myself in the reflection of a shop window. I didn't often look at my own image, so I tried to see myself as a stranger might. I was of middling height – only slightly above average for a man of this time. I was lean from a childhood of meager food, but strong from a youth spent climbing walls and escaping irate shopkeepers. My jaw had squared sometime in the last few years when I hadn't been paying attention except to shave it, my cheekbones were sharp enough to be considered patrician, and my tawny-colored hair had been looked after by my wife since we married, so it was a presentable shape and length. She had also kept my wardrobe, and despite the fashionably ridiculous cravats, I appeared perfectly respectable, if not fairly well-to-do.

In my own mind, however, I still felt like the grubby-capped, nimble-fingered street urchin I'd been before the world had opened and spit a girl into my time who didn't belong there. The simple acquisition of a twenty-first-century electric torch was a life-altering event that quite literally sparked my fascination with technology, past, present, and future.

I met Jess's eyes in the reflection of the window and nodded. "Let's go hear what Mr. Wilson has to say about his blackmailer, shall we?"

"And then to Scotland Yard?"

I nodded. "I anticipate a visit with Barings Bank as well. I'm going to have to put on my most pompous Eton accent to pull this off, you realize," I said in exactly that sort of posh, upper class accent I'd learned to mimic.

"Use the voice too – the deep one. That'll scare 'em into forgettin' to see 'ow young ye are."

I grinned at her. "You've discovered my secret weapon."

She rolled her eyes. "No, yer secret weapon is that ye're from the street."

"Ah, good point."

We'd arrived to find the pawnshop open for business, and Mr. Wilson wringing his hands nervously when we entered. "There you are," he mumbled.

"Take us down to your cellar, Mr. Wilson," I said, practicing the posh voice I'd need for my interviews with the police and the bank manager.

It must have worked, because Wilson didn't even hesitate. "Yes, sir. Come this way."

Jess shot me a smirk behind his back as he turned down a hall toward the cellar door.

Even in the dim light of a lantern, it was easy to see the scatterings of fresh dirt from the excavation that had recently taken place. "But – but – but I don't understand," Mr. Wilson sputtered when he saw the neat hole in one wall. "Who would dig a hole into my cellar?"

"Not into, Mr. Wilson, out from." I knelt to examine the tracks in the dirt. There were scuff marks where dirt had obviously been shoveled into bags and dragged out. "Do you have a garden in back of the shop?"

"Not a proper one," he said in some confusion. "It's more of a dirt patch, really."

I caught Jess's eye and jerked my head to the stairs. She understood my unspoken request and scampered up them immediately. She was back in less than two minutes, barely out of breath.

"A big pile of dirt against the back wall, with pieces of brick and mortar mixed in. It's enough to guess they got through."

"They?" asked Wilson, even more confused. "They who? And where did they get through?"

I stood up from my examination of the marks in the dirt. "At least two men dug this hole during the six weeks you were copying the *Encyclopaedia Britannica* for the redheaded woman."

166

"For the woman?" Wilson interrupted. "No, it was for the club."

"No, it was for the woman. This, here, is the print of a woman's shoe. The only person you ever saw was a woman, and if I had to guess, your blackmailer is very likely connected to her. Tell me about the blackmail, please."

Even in the dim lantern light, it was possible to see how thoroughly Mr. Wilson had paled. He heaved a beleaguered sigh and began his tale. "A widow came in two months ago, and I sold her a necklace. It was one that I'd had in my shop for several years. The widow came back the next day with a jeweler's report that the necklace had been part of a jewel heist several years before. The jeweler was willing to forget having seen the necklace, she said, but it would cost me fifteen pounds a month for six months, after which time he would return the original report to me to destroy."

"And this widow who bought the necklace? What can you tell me about her?"

Mr. Wilson looked blankly at me, and I tried again. "How did you determine that she was a widow?" I prompted.

He appeared somewhat confused, as though I should know this answer. "She was in mourning, and she always wore a black hat and veil when she was in my shop."

"Of course she did," I said finally. Which meant that this decidedly unobservant man had had even less opportunity to notice the woman's features than usual.

"Right, then," I breathed deeply to dispel growing frustration, "how do you make the payments?"

"The widow comes for them once a week to take to the jeweler," he said sullenly.

I doubted very highly that the widow took the payments anywhere at all, but there was finally something I might use. "And when is she expected again?"

"She was supposed to come yesterday, but she never did. Her money is still sitting right here." Mr. Wilson held up an envelope with a name written on it. I held my hand out for it, and after a slight hesitation, he gave it to me.

"Mrs. MacFarlane," I read out loud. "This is the woman's name?"

"It's what was on the bank draft with which she paid for the necklace."

"What else was on the draft? A first name perhaps? An address?"

He shook his head. "I didn't look beyond the bank name and the surname to cash it."

I took another deep breath. Was it possible to wander through life with so little curiosity? "From which bank was the draft drawn?"

He nodded toward hole in the wall. "Barings, just round the corner."

Jess caught my eye again, but Wilson didn't even seem to realize he'd just pointed in the direction of his new tunnel.

I brushed the dust off my hands and took the lantern with me toward the stairs. "Well, Mr. Wilson, I believe you've seen the last of the blackmailer. I also believe the necklace was never part of any heist, nor was it stolen at all. You've been duped into paying your own salary for the Redheaded League in order to get you out of the way while two men and a woman dug a tunnel from your cellar to that of Barings Bank."

"Club," he groused.

I looked at him in confusion. "Pardon me?"

"You said Redheaded League. It's a club," Wilson said with some satisfaction, as though the mistake vindicated his own shortcomings as a witness.

I looked him straight in the eyes and said with perhaps the beginnings of compassion, "It is nothing, Mr. Wilson. It was an elaborate scheme designed to remove you – one redheaded man with a conveniently placed business – from your shop. There is no Redheaded Club or League or anything else. There is a redheaded woman who may or may not be named MacFarlane—" As soon as I said it, I paused in shock. A redhead named MacFarlane? Could it be?

Jess scowled at me, and I continued after barely a pause. "A redheaded woman with an extraordinarily devious mind and a plot to steal from a bank. I will return shortly with a Metropolitan police officer and a manager of Barings Bank. Please don't leave your shop until then. And—" I said as an afterthought, "if you do indeed sell the pawnshop in Marylebone, I would appreciate if you came to me first. In exchange for that courtesy, I intend to remain silent on the matter of the blackmail in all conversations with the Metropolitan police. You are, of course, under no obligation to sell it at all, but I wanted to make my interest clear. Do we have an understanding?" He nodded, but possibly only because I gave him no choice. "Excellent. I bid you good day, sir."

Jess and I took our leave before Mr. Wilson had the presence of mind to protest, or indeed, to say anything at all.

Chapter 20 – The Lascar's Child

When we'd turned the corner onto Bishopsgate, Jess said, "Who's the woman?"

She startled me out of my thoughts. "Sorry?"

"You said *a redhead named MacFarlane* like you knew 'er. Who is she?"

"I don't actually know her. But I did know a redheaded man named Darrell MacFarlane once. He was a Scottish thief, and if this woman is somehow related to him, she is considerably more dangerous than even her cleverness would suggest."

We made our way to the Bishopsgate police station, and in remarkably short order convinced an officer to accompany us to Barings. The bank manager was only slightly less willing to show us the cellar of the bank, until he realized I intended to take the officer through the cellar of the pawnshop, and therefore it would be in his best interest to accompany us.

Mr. Wilson waited upstairs, as instructed, while I showed Officer Grant and Mr. Matlock the tunnel in the cellar. Officer Grant insisted on holding his cudgel at the ready, though I tried to tell him that the criminals were long gone. Mr. Matlock had somewhat more sense, and he led the way down the tunnel with a lantern in one hand and the set of determination in his shoulders.

The cellar of Barings Bank was a revelation to me because it was not, in fact, the vault. It was a storage room for filing cabinets, which Mr. Matlock began opening and closing in seemingly random order.

"If you will allow me, Mr. Matlock," I said curtly, in the voice designed to get his attention.

He stopped his search, and I took a moment to study the underground space by the light of my lantern. The floor and walls were brick, and some of the broken bricks left by the tunnelers were still scattered on the floor. There were tracks of brick dust to several of the cabinets. I examined the floor in front of each one of them until I found what I was looking for.

"Here," I said, pointing to a cabinet against the far wall.

It seemed to me that Mr. Matlock blanched. He knew what was supposed to be in there, and if it were missing, it looked as though there would be trouble.

He opened the cabinet drawer with a tremoring hand. The drawer was half-empty, as I suspected, and as he feared. Mr. Matlock visibly sagged against the wall.

"Oh no," he said quietly.

I quickly glanced at the remaining files for clues.

"What is it, sir? What's been taken?" asked Officer Grant.

"The files on Barings' investments in Argentina." Mr. Matlock said, almost absently. His mind seemed to be spinning, even as he began to wave the others out of the room.

I stood my ground, firmly planted on both feet. "Why would someone go to this immense trouble to steal your bank's files on Argentine investments?" It was less question and more command, and Mr. Matlock paled again.

"I'm sorry, I can't answer that," he said weakly.

Officer Grant didn't like that and decided to take a stand next to me. "Well, if you want the Met's help with any of this, you'd best be telling us why we're helping."

Mr. Matlock was near tears. "I can't. It's so far above my position, I shouldn't even know what I know."

"What do you know, Mr. Matlock?" I said it gently, because the fear in the man's eyes was real.

He whispered, "Barings is overextended, and most of it is in high-risk loans to Argentina."

Matlock seemed to come back to his senses, and he directed us out of the cellar and back through the tunnel into the pawnshop. "Officer, if you could perhaps post a guard until we've had a mason in to secure the bricks?" he asked Grant.

"I'll see to it," said Officer Grant in a serious tone.

Mr. Matlock shook my hand gravely. "Mr. Devereux, I thank you. If there's ever anything—"

"There is," I interrupted. "A woman named MacFarlane may be involved in all this. If there's anything at all that you discover about her, I would appreciate the information."

I handed him the calling card Charlie had made up for me a few months before. It said simply, *Devereux, Grayson House, Marylebone.* I liked it because a person had to work a little to find me.

I said my goodbyes and left Mr. Wilson to tell his tale to Officer Grant. He still looked bewildered, but I consoled myself that there was nothing criminal in his befuddlement; it was merely aggravating to anyone who needed the slightest bit of information from him.

Jess was outside the pawnshop, and we fell into step with each other as we walked. It wasn't far to Rothschild's Bank, so I bought Jess a cup of chocolate and asked her to wait near the cart outside the bank. The Rothschild's receptionist, Mrs. Blackburn, knew me from previous visits, and she sent me up the elevator to Aeris, Mr. Rothschild's personal assistant.

"Right this way, Mr. Devereux. Mr. Rothschild will be with you in a moment," Aeris said cheerfully.

I waited in Mr. Rothschild's office, which overlooked St. Swithin's Lane from its second floor window. A few minutes later, the banker entered his office with a smile and an extended hand.

174

"Mr. Devereux. It's always nice to see you."

"Thank you, Mr. Rothschild. It's a pleasure to see you as well."

"We are in contact with your estate agent about the Baker Street property, and everything is on schedule for the purchase."

"Ah, excellent. Thank you. It's not why I've come though."

"A message today for the safety deposit box then?" he asked, referring to the manner in which Charlie and I were able to get messages to Saira and Archer in their time. Rothschild's Bank would still be in existence, in this very location, in more than a hundred years, so it was a secure means of sending messages to a place and time no telegraph or telephone could reach.

"Actually, no. I may very well be breaking a confidentiality, but as I was not asked to keep the information a secret, I will accept the risk." I then proceeded to describe the circumstances that led to the Argentine files being stolen from Barings Bank, and the fear of the bank manager when he described Barings' overextension in their investments.

Mr. Rothschild listened solemnly, and when I was finished, he rose and shook my hand with genuine warmth. "Mr. Devereux, what you've told me is of great concern. If indeed Barings is overextended in Argentina, and if those files were stolen by someone who means to do the bank harm, it would take very little to set an Argentine economic crisis in motion, which could in turn, cause the collapse of Barings and much of England's financial market as well. I appreciate what you've told me and will address it with Barings and the Bank of England immediately. Between us, we will do what we can to prop them up to avert a crisis."

He walked me to the door and opened it for me. "Please give my regards to your lovely wife, and I offer you my sincerest thanks for this information."

"May I give you another bit of information?" I said as I stepped into the hall where Aeris held the elevator for me.

"Of course," he said.

"If a woman named MacFarlane is a client of your bank, possibly a widow, possibly with red hair, please be aware of her activity. I consider her to be a person of interest in this Barings business."

"I will look into it," Rothschild nodded.

Jess waited outside the bank wearing the slightest hint of a chocolate mustache. I didn't tell her about it or wipe it off. It actually suited her messenger boy disguise.

"See? I said ye were a toff, didn't I? Bankin' at Rothschild's." She snorted in disgust, and I laughed.

"It is rather ridiculous, isn't it?"

She looked sideways at me and seemed to find comfort in the fact that I could laugh at myself. "Right, well, a person 'as to 'ave two coins to rub together to keep one in a bank."

"Do you want to open an account here? We're paying you weekly, and it'll be more than two coins." To be honest, I had no idea what sort of payment deal Charlie had worked out with Jess, but if anything, she was far more generous than I knew how to be.

She scoffed, but she didn't say no, and I needed to remember to make a trip back here after Jess had been paid.

We walked in silence for a few minutes. Although Bishopsgate to Marylebone was no small distance, I preferred walking to almost every other form of transportation around London. It allowed me to notice the small things about the neighborhoods we traversed – to notice who kept flowers in their window boxes, and who left refuse in the streets. Pride in one's home said much about one's general contentment and sense of belonging to a place. And those neighborhoods where people swept sidewalks and neighbors greeted each other by name seemed to have fewer hungry children on their streets.

It also allowed me to notice the mood of my companion, which had shifted from observant and aware to quietly thoughtful. Jess's voice did not, therefore, surprise me when she finally spoke. "I was born not far from 'ere, in a tiny flat on Love Lane near St. Mary's on the 'Ill. My mother worked for a fishmonger at Billingsgate Market, and my da was a lascar on a fishin' boat for the Crown. I lived with 'er and 'er brother, but I saw my da twice a year before 'e went missin'. 'E used to carry me on 'is shoulder and tell me stories in a language I didn't understand, and 'e taught me to run, and 'ow to 'ide from the toughs that roamed the lanes around the docks. My mother liked 'im well enough when 'e was there, but she cursed 'im somethin' awful when 'e didn't come back. 'Er brother married, and the new wife didn't like a half-color brat in 'er 'ouse, so we were put out."

She faltered, and I kept my eyes on the street to give her time to finish her thought. "My mother tried to put me in an orphanage, but I ran away. The last time I saw 'er she 'ad only 'alf 'er teeth, and 'er pretty face was scarred with pox. She didn't recognize me, and I was glad."

Jess said nothing else for a long time, and I didn't think she'd appreciate words just to fill the silent spaces, so I kept my thoughts to myself. "She blamed my da for 'ow I look, but she liked 'im well enough to lay with 'im, so maybe it was just me she didn't want."

I was about to reply when her next words kicked me in the stomach.

"I hate my da for makin' me brown and then leavin' me to 'er."

I took a deep breath to calm the storm that threatened to boil over, and I felt my accent slip into one with well-worn edges and faded colors, like the childhood memories that I'd worked so hard to banish. "My own ma died when I was 'alf yer age, and if she knew my da, she never said."

178

Jess darted a glance at me, surprised, perhaps, that I was speaking of myself. She said nothing though, and I continued. "For the first five years of my life, I was cold and 'ungry, but I didn't know any different, so it didn't count for much. But she loved me, my ma did, and for a time after she died, I 'ated her for it."

The memory of that hatred could still double me over with echoed pain, and I made a point to keep breathing so I could continue. "She showed me 'er love in a 'undred little ways — tuckin' the 'air behind my ear, answerin' even the smallest question. And there's a thing a mother does when ye 'ave a smudge on yer cheek?" I licked the tip of my thumb and pretended to reach for Jess's face. She ducked automatically, but her eyes went wide.

"Me da used to do that to me."

I nodded. "That's love. Teachin' ye 'ow to survive like yer da did, that's love too. My ma used to read to me every mornin' when the sun came up and there was light to read by. We'd lay 'uddled under a blanket, not ready to face the cold day, 'er voice whisperin' the words in my ear. She gave me 'er love of words, and she made me wonder about things, and when she died, I was still 'ungry and cold — that 'adn't changed — but suddenly there was no one to wipe my cheek, and no one readin' me words anymore."

"Ye read to yerself now, though," Jess said.

I smiled, and the accent faded from my speech with the closing of my memories. "And every time I do, I'm reminded that my mother loved me."

We walked in silence for a few minutes. "Do ye still 'ate 'er?" she finally asked.

"No. And for the record, your father's love was a gift that had nothing to do with your mother's failings." I didn't stop to face her, though I wanted to. I wanted to see her eyes when I said the words I believed to be true. "I know plenty of people, rich or poor, black or brown or white, who weren't wanted by the people who birthed them. Who you come from and what you look like — that's just an accident of your parents' choices. What you *do* with the hair color, skin color, strength, cleverness, and speed you've got, that's *your* choice. You get to choose if you are a poor, brown girl, or if you're a strong, smart, wily, brown girl with sharp eyes and quick wits."

"I use my brown skin to 'ide in dark places, like my da taught me to."

I nodded. "I used to have to hide under a thick layer of dirt or my skin would practically glow in gaslight."

She giggled, and it was a nice sound. "Not very useful, white skin, is it?"

I shrugged. "It's useful for blending into England's upper class, but no, not very practical for doing the things that really interest me."

"Is there a place in the world where the upper class is brown?" she asked.

"Lots of them. There are even places where everyone is brown. But like every other accident of birth, color is one of the least useful measures for deciding the quality of a person. There's no merit involved in being brown or white, or male or female for that matter, and bestowing rank and privilege for birth accidents is rather like congratulating an egg for the color of its shell."

We walked in silence for a few minutes, past a bookseller that I might have stopped in at if I'd been alone. I sensed that Jess needed to examine my words for cracks and holes, and perhaps try them on to see how they fit.

"What about the people who only see the poor brown girl when they look at me?" she finally asked.

"What about them?" I said with a shrug and no trace of sarcasm.

She scowled, and I finally stopped and raised her chin with my finger so she'd meet my eyes. "*You* are the only person who can ever truly determine your worth. No one else has that power unless you give it to them."

She met my gaze squarely and didn't back down. "Why do ye think I chose the friends I did?"

I couldn't bite back the smile, but I let go of her chin and continued walking. "Why?"

"Because they know who I am. They see what I do, and they believe what I say."

"Then they're your family," I said with complete certainty.

She spoke so quietly I almost didn't catch the words. "And now ye are too."

Chapter 21 – Home Life

It took several days for the estate agents, lawyers, and bankers to hash out an agreement for the Baker Street building, and in the meantime, Charlie and I spent a considerable amount of time each day teaching children.

Our irregulars were a hungry bunch – food, information, knowledge, experience – they inhaled it all. Reesy was very often glued to Mrs. Mac's side. He had a fascination with the house, the maintenance and running of it, and especially what went on in the kitchen. He had a natural gift for adding just the right herb or odd ingredient to a dish that would take it from very good to remarkable. Mrs. Mac was delighted with Reesy's company and happy to teach him everything her own father, the butler in a grand estate, had taught her about keeping a home.

Hannah was a tiny girl, likely of part-African heritage, with a spread of brown freckles across her cheeks, bright green eyes, and curly black hair. If not for her eyes, she would fade into the background quite completely, as she made no noise at all, and she could sit still for hours at the window watching the birds in the sky. She loved Charlie's drawings though, and I began to take care that I didn't accidentally trip over her small form, arms curled around her knees, on the floor in front of them. She seemed difficult to reach at first, until Charlie sketched a small portrait of Hannah's face. The gleam of tears in Hannah's eyes was louder than any words of thanks could ever be, and after that, she was never without a pencil and a sketchbook. Her drawings were crude at first, but there was always one element that shone brighter than the rest, and Charlie began working with the girl to help her find the light in every picture, and in herself.

Jess and little Oliver were most often with me – Jess by my side, watching whatever I did, and Oliver underfoot, trying to thwart us. Jess was so clever she regularly shocked me with her grasp of new concepts. She was also prickly and sensitive, but her growing trust in us made her withdrawals fewer and farther between. Reading came quickly to Jess, although every word that she learned to read became a song to Oliver, until his perseveration made everyone in the house half-mad with his music in their ears. But the madness was useful when it came time to teach numbers. There was no better way to learn multiplication facts than to turn them into a song, and since no one could get his music out of their brain, all four children had learned their times-tables by heart in four days.

Oliver was reciting the periodic table to the tune of the alphabet while Jess and I were experimenting with magnets in one of the unused butler's pantries when Hannah came running to find us. She signed something to Jess too quickly for me to see, then raced back up to the main floor. "The big Irishman is here to see you," Oliver translated before Jess could get the iron pins out of her mouth.

"The big Irishman has come to *find* you," Oscar Wilde boomed from the open doorway. I was connecting a tricky bit of wiring and couldn't look up from my work, but I could hear amusement in Oscar's tone.

"The workshop is definitely a no-jacket zone, Wilde. I'm not sure you're quite prepared for how savage we actually are in this household," I said, giving the wire a final twist with the pliers. "There, it's done." I looked up at Jess holding the lantern. "I thank you for the light."

"What on earth are you doing, Devereux? It's positively medieval in here."

"Playing Dr. Frankenstein," I said with a smile.

"Oddly, the role suits you," he laughed. "And who are these lovely minions?" He regarded Jess and Oliver with frank curiosity, and I could tell he didn't recognize Jess as the pickpocket from the Langham Hotel.

185

"My Igors. Jess, Oliver, meet Mr. Oscar Wilde." Jess was drawing a schematic of the wires we'd just connected, so she merely glanced up with a nod. "Sir." She looked a little more closely. "Ye need a new mantle on yer gaslight. The one on the right burns brighter than the left, and ye've clipped yer sideburns crooked."

I bit back a laugh at the expression on Wilde's face. "Good God, man, is everyone in this house as extraordinary as you and the lovely Mrs. Devereux?"

He peered at Oliver as if for confirmation and jumped back, slightly startled. Oliver grinned broadly, and I wondered if he'd seen a pointed canine glinting in the lamplight. "He's ... he's ..."

"Part *other*. Charlie thinks he's most likely from the lesser fae." Jess glanced up at Oscar to see his reaction to my words. We had shown the children Charlie's drawing of Oliver's true face, and they'd studied it for a second, studied him for two, and then run off to play a hide-and-seek game of dwarves versus elves.

"Quite," Wilde said with interest, and Jess seemed satisfied. With effort, he drew his eyes away from Oliver and turned the full weight of his smile back to me. "Conan Doyle seems to think you've been solving mysteries again."

I raised an eyebrow. "Really? I wonder where he gets his information."

"Apparently he has an old friend in the Met, and they seemed quite taken aback at the ease with which you discovered the

186

robbery of Barings Bank. There's talk of asking you to consult with them from time to time on some of their more difficult cases."

I scoffed. "I'm certain Scotland Yard needs no help from me."

Wilde shook his head. "Not so, not so. After that Whitechapel business with the Ripper last year, I do believe their confidence has been shaken."

I winced. I knew far more about that Whitechapel business than I could ever admit to, and I definitely did not need to come to the notice of men who had been looking for the killer.

"They say you believe a woman is behind the crime," Oscar continued.

Jess caught my eye, and I could see the question in them. *Do you trust him?*

The fact was, I did trust Oscar. He was loud and brash, and he delighted in inciting chaos just to see which way people would run, but I trusted that his heart was good and his mind was brilliant. I also decided that it was time for me to allow the truth to reveal some pieces of me I'd thus far kept hidden – from Oscar, and from Jess.

"Oliver, run up to Charlie and ask her to set a place for Mr. Wilde. I believe he might join us for our evening meal."

Oliver got up and said to Wilde in perfectly clear speech, "You'll like it. Reesy's making cottage pie, and he adds bacon."

The boy's intonation was a perfect imitation of Wilde's own speech, and the fact that it came from a boy the size of a toddler was quite shocking to my friend. He stared after him until Jess quietly got up to go to the door. She looked at me for direction.

"Stay please, Jess."

She nodded and closed the door behind Oliver, then came back to the work table to sit.

I settled myself on a stool and bid Oscar to do the same. "I do believe a woman is behind this, but of greater concern to me is that it is slightly possible that I know her family."

"Why is that of concern?" asked Wilde.

"Because she may be a Monger mix." I exhaled quietly, trusting that Wilde would know what I meant. From the slight widening of his eyes, it seemed he did.

Jess, however, did not. "What's a Monger?"

I opened my mouth with absolutely no idea what I was going to say, but Oscar interrupted me.

"There are those people you sometimes encounter that you just know in your bones are schemers and troublemakers. Now imagine a whole family line that began very long ago with a master schemer whose descendants all carry this propensity for plotting mayhem. The descendants of that family are called Mongers, and the scheming and plotting are very real skills they inherited from their powerful ancestor."

Jess digested this information surprisingly well, and she turned her attention back to me. "So if the woman is a Monger, it means she 'as extra criminal skills."

"Yes, that's likely. But the larger point is," and I looked at Oscar as I continued, "if she is indeed related to a young man I once knew named Darrell MacFarlane, things might be more complicated beyond just her Monger heritage."

Wilde studied me. "Because ...?"

"Darrell was a highlander, a thief, and a mixed-blood Monger ... who could travel in time."

CHAPTER 22 – TIME

Jess stared at me blankly while Oscar laughed out loud.

"I'm not sure which is worse – the fact he's a thief, a Clocker mix, or a highlander," Oscar said with complete sincerity.

Jess snapped her mouth shut and spun to face Wilde. "Bein' a thief 'as much to recommend it."

"I can't disagree with her," I said smiling.

Oscar inclined his head to her. "I bow to your superior understanding of such matters, young lady. Forgive me."

"What's a Clocker?" she said in response.

This time Oscar looked to me to answer the question. I forged ahead. "In the same way the Mongers have their ancestor's trouble-making skills, so do the Clockers have variations on their ancestor's ability to travel in time."

Her eyes narrowed. "I don't understand 'travel in time.' What does that mean?"

I sighed. The story I'd avoided telling was the simplest means to communicate the concept. "A few years ago, when I was still thieving for my living, I met a girl with strange clothes and a strange way about her. I helped her, and we became friends of a sort, and before she left, she gave me a device from her time."

"A device … from her time?" Jess asked hesitantly. I had Oscar's full attention as well, since this was not part of any story he had ever heard.

"Saira gave me her torch. It was an electric light that she held in her hand like a wand."

"Magic?" Jess breathed.

"It seemed so to me at the time. But since then I've been to Saira's time, and devices such as the electric torch are commonplace then, as are the batteries that power it."

"When, exactly, is Saira's time?" Oscar asked.

"More than a century from now."

He exhaled, but said nothing. Jess's eyes gleamed in the dim gaslight, and she practically whispered the words, "You've been there?"

I nodded and assessed her understanding of the magnitude of what I had just revealed. She seemed to be absorbing this concept like she did everything else – fully, and without judgement.

Oscar looked around my makeshift workshop, and his gaze lingered on the generator motor I was attempting to wire. "You've seen the wonders of the future—" he began.

"—And they will remain in the future," I finished for him. "I am merely attempting to invent the things which are being invented by others now, using available technology and materials."

Oscar smiled and tapped a finger to his head. "A little bit of knowledge can go a long way, eh, Devereux?"

I'd been holding myself very tightly since the conversation began, and some of the tension began to seep away. "It's remarkable what an eidetic memory can accomplish when given the right tools."

"What's an eidetic memory?" Jess asked, looking to both of us for the answer.

"The ability to take a mental photograph of something and then "see" a perfect recreation of the memory at will," Oscar explained.

"Oh. I can do that," Jess said dismissively.

Oscar raised an eyebrow at me across the top of Jess's head. I just grinned. "Of course you can," I said.

"I want to know what happens in the future," Jess insisted.

"You will. Each day you live, you're learning what happens in the future." She scowled, I laughed, and Oscar regarded us both with an amused smile.

"It is rather tempting to know. When I realized that the lovely Saira knew my work, it was all I could do not to probe for the juicy bits of gossip about my life, my fame, and my fortune."

I knew what he was asking and kept my expression as neutral as possible as I thought about the ignoble end of Oscar Wilde. "I wish for us all a life full of love, laughter, and the wisdom to pursue whatever creative endeavors feed our souls."

It didn't fool him for a minute, though Wilde raised an imaginary glass in a toast. "Hear, hear!"

Jess watched us pretend joviality neither of us felt, then she said, "When do we go lookin' for the red'eaded woman?"

"She's a ginger?" Wilde asked.

"Apparently, a flaming redhead." My words brought to mind the image of Leighton's *Flaming June* painting, but I shoved it away. "Beyond noticing the woman's red hair, our primary witness has the approximate observational skills of an oak plank," I grumbled.

"He can't have been the only one to see her though?"

I exhaled. "I've been avoiding the prospect of searching for witnesses. It really has nothing to do with me, and certainly no one has asked me to look into it."

Wilde looked me straight in the eyes. "You should look into it. If, as you suspect, the woman is of the Monger persuasion, this was not an isolated crime. She is by nature a Machiavellian schemer, and I suggest it would be best to know as much about her as you can before you actually come face-to-face with her in a dark alley somewhere.""I'm good in dark alleys," I mumbled in a surly tone. I *knew* I should investigate further, and it certainly wouldn't take much time, but I'd resisted doing anything at all that could be construed as Sherlockian. As it was, I knew it was historically inevitable that Conan Doyle would get wind of the story of the Redheaded Men's Club and turn it into *The Redheaded League* for The Strand magazine.

"Of course you're good in dark alleys. Shall I join you in my pink and green frock coat, or can you be trusted to investigate without my fashion sense to brighten those alleys for you?"

I smirked. "I almost want to see you in the pink and green frock coat. I would have to wear a burgundy cravat to clash loudly and painfully with your wardrobe."

"You wouldn't dare!" Wilde said in mock horror.

Jess shoved her stool back and stood. "Why ye two are on about frocks when there's Mongers about, I don't understand!"

"We don't know she's a Monger," I cautioned.

"And ye won't until we find 'er, and maybe not even then. I'm goin' for supper. Reesy's bacon cottage pie's not to be missed, and I can't listen to talk about pink, green, or burgundy a minute longer."

She stomped up the stairs dramatically, and Oscar sighed. "It pains me."

"What does?" I asked as I cleaned up the work table.

"To be no longer young enough to know everything."

Chapter 23 – The College of Arms

Mr. Carrigan was the owner of the building where Mr. Wilson went to copy the *Encyclopaedia Britannica* every day for six weeks. He was an older gentleman, quite hard of hearing who carried an amplifying horn in one hand and a massive ring of keys in his pocket. There were six offices to let on a monthly basis, he explained to me as Jess loitered within earshot nearby, and four were currently occupied. The room in which Mr. Wilson had spent his days was let for two months and paid for in advance. The name on the lease was listed as A. Westfield, whose secretary had taken possession of the keys and then returned them in an envelope pushed under the door.

"What did the secretary look like?" I inquired of Mr. Carrigan. He put the amplifying horn to his ear and asked me to please repeat my question.

"The secretary who received the keys — what did she look like?" I said louder.

"Not often you find a female secretary, and a pretty one at that. Makes one wonder why there's no husband to object."

I bit back the twenty-first century response that statement deserved and concentrated on getting information. "How old was she?"

"Old enough to know better, I say," Mr. Carrigan grumbled.

Right. I inhaled deeply to steady my temper and tried again. "Can you tell me how tall she was, or the color of her hair?"

"Her hair. Well, now, that was red — as red as raspberries. It was the brightest thing in the room, it was."

Excellent. "And her eyes, her skin tone? Her approximate build?"

Mr. Carrigan made a brusque motion with one hand. "Who could notice anything else when that hair came in. She wore the mass of curls long, as a maiden might. It was downright distracting. I wanted to tie it up into a knot just so it would stop waving at me like so many snakes. If she hadn't taken the keys from my hand, I might have forgotten I even had them, her hair had charmed me so."

Well, that was new — distraction by hair. A woman, able to render men blind and senseless by virtue of a nest of writhing curls. It seemed a double-edged sword though — a man couldn't describe a face he didn't see, but the hair, spotted anywhere on the streets of London, would be unmistakable.

"Is there anything else you can tell me about the redheaded woman, Mr. Carrigan? Any detail, no matter how small?"

"Well, I don't know how important a thing this is, but the woman came in a carriage with a crest on it. She seemed in a hurry too, as though it were just one stop of many that she had to make."

"Did you, by chance, recognize the crest?" That seemed a foolish thing for the woman to do – to travel in an identifiable conveyance seemed the height of carelessness for one so seemingly clever.

"I did not. It was a letter M entwined around a stag's horns."

The man couldn't see a female face in front of him, but he could identify the design of a crest on a carriage outside his building? It didn't bear examination. Mr. Carrigan began rattling the keys in his pocket, his patience for my questions clearly at an end.

"Thank you so much for your time, Mr. Carrigan. I bid you a good day."

Jess slipped up next to me as I walked away from the building. "'E was a right old codger, wasn't 'e?"

"I very nearly launched into a lecture on the rights of women, but I opted to seek information from him instead."

She shrugged. "Would've been wasted breath. The information ye got was good and worth the bitten tongue."

"Agreed. We need to find that crest." I turned south and aimed us toward Queen Victoria Street. "I've never had occasion to visit the College of Arms. This should be interesting."

"What's the College of Arms?" Jess asked.

"It is technically part of the queen's household, though it has a corporate charter and is overseen by the Duke of Norfolk. It maintains the records for all of the aristocracy of England, Wales, and Ireland. The library in the College of Arms houses every coat of arms, and the heralds who work there have been keeping genealogies and records for every noble family since the time of King Richard III."

"So the toffs with titles 'ave someone else keepin' their family books?"

I nodded. "Probably only the male descendants though, since most hereditary titles can only pass through the men."

Jess scoffed. "Doesn't foster much need for daughters, does it?"

"It would rather simplify things if titles could be bestowed on the person best-suited to the duties rather than by virtue of birth order and gender." I smirked and added, "Though it's probably not wise to say so out loud on my way into the College of Arms."

Jess looked up at the imposing, U-shaped brick building at which we'd arrived. She scanned the façade quickly, and then tapped my arm and gestured to one wing. "There's a door for the 'elp. I'll go look for a way into the storage room in case we need it later?"

I nodded. "We'll meet back here in one hour."

She peeled off toward the service door in the east wing, and I marched resolutely through the gates to the front door. The reception room was paneled in beautiful wood and looked as though it had remained unchanged for two hundred years. An older man with a young one, whom I presumed to be father and son, stood near one wall speaking quietly amongst themselves. A portly young man, a few years older than I, entered the room and greeted me with a smile.

"How can I help you, sir?" he said to me brightly.

The trepidation I'd felt about asking to search the records of the peerage loosened its hold on my voice, and I matched my smile to his.

"A coat of arms was described to me, and I would like to discover to whom it belongs. How would I go about doing so?"

"I'd be happy to provide you with the scrolls Mr.—"

"Devereux."

He shook my hand. "Mr. Devereux. I'm Percy Hunt, and it is my pleasure to serve here as an archivist. Would that be Archer Devereux?"

The question startled me with its unexpectedness. "No, it's Ringo."

I wasn't normally in the habit of giving my first name, and I'd never before encountered someone who had mistaken me for Saira's husband. Archer Devereux had given me his last name as my own, but he had left London some months before and was currently somewhere in the north of England. I didn't have more than a moment to consider the coincidence that Percy knew my name though, because he was moving toward a staircase at the rear of the building.

"Come, Mr. Devereux, I'll take you upstairs to a work room and bring some reference books for you to study."

He led me up the winding steps, past several portraits of men I assumed must have been past heralds, to the third floor. The wood creaked beneath our feet as we moved down a long hallway lined with doors. Percy knocked lightly on a door. When there was no answer, he opened it and peered inside. A table and two chairs were the only furniture, with a large gaslamp suspended overhead.

"Please make yourself comfortable. I shall return in just a few minutes with the books of crests."

I had just taken myself on a thorough tour of the room's shelves, cabinets, and one hidden cubby under the table in which a forty-year-old half-finished love letter to *Lady Dorothy* lay forgotten, when Percy knocked lightly and opened the door. He carried two large, heavy, leather-bound books in his arms, which he maneuvered through the doorway and onto the table. He was huffing slightly, but the smile remained a regular part of his expression.

"There you go, Mr. Devereux. That should keep you busy for the next several hours, unless you get lucky and the crest you seek is one of the old families."

"They're arranged chronologically then?" I asked, eyeing the thick books with reluctance.

He grimaced charmingly. "Yes, I'm sorry. These books are merely the registers of the coats of arms. There was no other way to record them than in order of creation. Now if you had come in with a family name seeking the accompanying crest, that would be recorded in a different volume altogether."

"The letter M is part of the design. Might that help?" I asked.

Percy thought for a moment. "I'll just nip down and pull the alphabetically ordered book for the M's then. I'll be only another moment."

Five minutes later he was back, with a sheen of sweat over his brow and a decided wheeze. "Here you go – the M's." He placed another, slimmer volume on the table, and then leaned against it to catch his breath.

"I truly appreciate your help, Mr. Hunt. Thank you so much."

"Of course, Mr. Devereux. It is my pleasure. I've taken the liberty of recording the time and date of your visit in the logs of the coats of arms registers. When you are finished, you may leave them on the table and show yourself out. I shall return them to

201

their place in the library after you've gone. If you are in need of any copies, you may bookmark those pages and I will have copies sent around to Grayson House."

My eyebrows jumped. "You know where I live?"

Percy winked as he wiped the sweat from his forehead. "We're archivists, Mr. Devereux. Every listing in our archives includes all known information, including homes, businesses, and families."

I struggled to maintain my composure at such an intriguing resource. "I had no idea that I was listed in your archives."

Percy looked incredulous. "Half-brother to Archer Devereux and fifth in line to the dukedom? Of course you are recorded at the College of Arms."

I think I managed to keep a neutral expression on my face, though I actually felt like laughing – or crying – I wasn't quite sure which. "Right. Of course," I murmured.

"Well then, I'll leave you to your search."

Percy closed the door softly behind him and walked away down the hall toward the stairs. I was utterly impressed with, and completely flummoxed by, the results of his quick investigation of me. Apparently, the records in the College of Arms could be very useful if ever I were to need information on the nobility. Fifth in line, indeed. I snorted to myself and pulled the "M" book toward me.

There was a scratch at the door, as if a mouse were in the walls. "Come in, Jess," I said quietly.

She slipped into the room and closed the door before I'd even finished saying the words.

She tossed her head in the direction of the stairs. "'E looked ye up in 'is big records book. I 'eard 'im talkin' to another toff, askin' if 'e knew when yer name 'ad been added. The other one said Archer Devereux added 'is brother a few months ago, and they just assumed ye must be the acknowledged get from the wrong side of the sheets."

Archer had added my name to the records, obviously. No one else could have, but the realization that he had done this without ever telling me was like discovering that Santa Clause was real and coming to dinner.

"You found the archives themselves?" I finally asked, when I'd gotten past the rather large frog that had taken up residence in my throat.

She grinned. "Wasn't 'ard to find. There aren't many people about either, so if ye ever need a book off the record …"

I shook my head at her with a smile. "Although my instinct is to sneak, I've learned it's generally much easier and safer to go in through the front door."

She snorted. "When ye're big, and rich, and a bloke – sure."

"Fair point."

I handed her one of the two coats of arms books. "Are your hands clean?" I asked.

She made a face at me and held up her hands for inspection. They were, in fact, very clean.

"We're lookin' for an M wound 'round stags 'orns, yeah?"

"Right." I opened the book of M-names and began turning the vellum pages. The book was beautifully illustrated with fine, hand-painted crests and calligraphy-inscribed family information. The first Duke of Marlborough, for example, had been John Churchill in the late 17th century, whose father, Winston Churchill was the ancestor and namesake of the man who would be prime minister in forty years. Marlborough's sister, Arabella, had been mistress to King James II and mother to four of his children. I could get lost in a book like this for hours.

A scant one hour later, after countless pages of beautifully intricate artwork, and far more secrets about the nobility than most people realized could be found in the pages of a genealogical book, I found it.

"Morcar," I said, more loudly than I intended to. I was surprised to see that name, but there was the beautifully curved M wrapped around the horns of a stag.

"The countess?" Jess asked, looking up from her book.

"The carbuncle." I confirmed.

We stared at each other for a long moment before I rubbed my eyes and exhaled. "I think we need Conan Doyle."

CHAPTER 24 – THE COUNTESS

Arthur Conan Doyle had responded promptly to my message and was seated at his usual table in the Langham Hotel dining room. I came to lunch alone, though Jess waited in the lobby in her messenger boy costume watching the entrance.

"Can you arrange a meeting for me with the Countess of Morcar?" I asked, after the proper pleasantries had been observed.

The Scot raised two bushy eyebrows in surprise. "I thought the business with the blue carbuncle was finished."

"The gem has been returned to her, but it seems she, or someone who works for her, may be involved in something else I'm looking into for Barings." I decided to drop the bank's name, despite having no official right to do so. It certainly got Conan Doyle's attention.

"I don't actually know the countess, you realize."

"You were the man who called Scotland Yard about the thief. Your name is perhaps the only one associated with her gemstone's return. I believe it's enough to get an audience with her."

Conan Doyle regarded me thoughtfully for a long moment. "If I do this for you, I'll need something in return."

I sighed. I knew this was coming. "The Redheaded League."

He sat forward, his full attention on my face. "Tell me."

So I told him – the simple version at least. I did not, however, go into any detail about the woman, or about the countess's coat of arms. Conan Doyle practically glowed with excitement.

"Why on earth did you stomp around on the sidewalk outside of the pawnshop?"

"Well, it seemed clear that someone needed the pawnshop to gain access to some other place. A tunnel seemed a logical conclusion to draw, but as the walk outside the front of the shop wasn't obviously hollow beneath, it seemed likely that the criminals were tunneling the other direction. A quick jaunt around the corner made it clear that Barings Bank was the objective."

"Remarkable. A tunnel."

I shrugged. "They only employed Mr. Wilson for six weeks. There are limited ways to utilize that access in such a short time. Digging was just the most obvious."

"Well, I'd love to hear what you would have looked for next if the criminals hadn't dug a tunnel," Conan Doyle said in wonder.

I merely smiled and said, "So, you'll contact the countess for me?"

A swift, light whistle caught my attention, and I stood to see Jess toss her head in the direction of a party that had just entered the hotel.

"Actually, she has just returned to the Langham. Might you be willing to invite her to sit with us?" I asked Conan Doyle, not taking my eyes off the woman and her young maid who had just entered the hotel.

Conan Doyle needed no more prompting than that. He strode out to the lobby and intercepted the countess before she could ring for the elevator. I followed a few feet behind him.

"Lady Morcar, if I might beg a moment of your time?" Conan Doyle was a tall, burly man, and his Scottish accent and large mustache gave him an air of gravity that seemed to impress the countess. She stopped and waited for him to continue.

He dipped his head in a courteous bow. "My name is Arthur Conan Doyle, and I wonder if my colleague and I might have a word with you regarding the incident of your blue carbuncle?"

She studied him carefully. Lady Morcar's silver hair was perfectly coiffed, and her silver fox stole was an identical match for it. There wasn't a bead or a bauble out of place, and nestled in the hollow of her throat was the blue carbuncle itself, hanging from a heavy silver chain.

"You are the one who insisted the doorman had nothing to do with the theft," she said in an imperious tone as she looked down her long nose at the man who was so much taller than she. He shifted uncomfortably under her scowling gaze, and then shot the merest glance in my direction as though willing me to come to his rescue. The countess saw the glance, and her glare turned in my direction for the space of a breath before she returned her eyes to Conan Doyle.

"I understand the gemstone was discovered to have merely been misplaced, not stolen," said Conan Doyle gravely.

The countess scoffed. "Come now, you don't actually believe it could have fallen in my teapot and stayed there unnoticed for a week." And then she did a most extraordinary thing. The countess winked. "Tell me who did steal my gem, and I will give you that moment." Her tone was still severe, but the wink had left a bright twinkle in her eyes, and I very nearly smiled in relief.

Conan Doyle did smile, and he indicated the way to the dining room. "Would you join myself and my colleague, Mr. Ringo Devereux, at our table?"

Lady Morcar studied the dining room with a critical eye. "I think not, Mr. Conan Doyle." My stomach clenched again, and I hoped I could draw her eye again for one last chance to ask a question before she stalked away. And then she did look at me with the full weight of her imperious gaze. "I believe you and Mr. Devereux shall knock on the door to my suite in precisely fifteen minutes, and we shall have tea in my rooms," she glanced at Conan Doyle to include him, "though I expect no more mysteriously-returned stones shall accost us." Conan Doyle barely suppressed a smile as he nodded.

"Certainly, my lady. It would be our pleasure."

Her eyes flicked back to me. "And if the boy is yours, she can eat with my maid."

With that astonishing statement, Lady Morcar swept out of the lobby without a backward glance. Her young maid fell in two steps behind her, carrying packages from what seemed to have been a shopping outing, and a moment later, they were in the elevator and gone.

Conan Doyle hadn't heard what she'd said to me, but Jess had edged close enough to us that she did. Her eyes met mine with worry, but I let her see the hint of a smile. If the countess was observant enough to spot Jess *and* determine her costume and gender, she would very likely be an excellent witness.

Exactly fifteen minutes later, Conan Doyle and I stood outside Lady Morcar's suite. Jess had taken the stairs and waited until we were admitted inside by the maid before she slipped in behind us. "Lady Morcar invites you to join her in the dining room," the maid said timidly. She was young and slender, but she looked us in the eye when she spoke to us, and she addressed Lady Morcar with a straight spine and an unwavering voice when she announced our presence to her.

I saw her give Jess a quick smile as she closed the dining room doors behind us, and I thought they might have a rather interesting conversation in the other room.

Lady Morcar was probably in her early fifties, with a regal bearing and the sort of manners that spoke of an utterly rigid upbringing. I doubted she had ever run wild in a field chasing dogs, and the image of it nearly brought a grin to my face. I composed myself quickly and greeted her with a bow when Conan Doyle had finished thanking her.

"I have not heard of you, Devereux, and yet I feel I must. Tell me why that is."

Conan Doyle answered when I hesitated. "He found your carbuncle, my lady, and it was also he who engineered its return to you."

Her glittering eyes sharpened on me. "Indeed." The one word was a command to explain, and so I did. She was silent throughout my recitation of the facts, and waited until I was finished with my tale to speak.

"So Catherine did it. I wondered."

"Your ladyship?"

"Catherine Cusack was my companion. The day you had the stone returned to me was the last day I saw her. She was extraordinary, and I've missed her every day she's been gone. Delilah is very good, of course," she nodded toward the other room where the young woman and Jess sat behind closed doors, "but she's very young."

"Your companion? I understood she was your maid," Conan Doyle observed gruffly.

Lady Morcar snapped at him. "She's far too well-educated to be anyone's maid."

"How long was she with you?" I asked.

"Only six months, though it seems like far longer. We became very close, you see. At least I presumed my affection was returned. Catherine was quick-witted, very observant, and remarkably intelligent. She knew when to hold her tongue, and she was an excellent source of information about enemies and friends alike."

"May I ask, my lady, in that time, did she have the use of your carriage?"

Lady Morcar looked startled by the question. "Of course she did. How else was she to do my personal business? On foot?" She said it as though walking were an unthinkable bore.

"For the six weeks prior to her departure, what were her working hours with you?"

The countess's gaze sharpened on my face, but she answered the question. "She had asked for a leave of absence for six weeks to take care of her ailing grandmother. I granted it of course, because I cared for Catherine … and I imagine I hoped she might one day care for me the same way. She had been back for a week

211

when the carbuncle was stolen, and a week after that, she was gone."

There was genuine pain in Lady Morcar's voice as she spoke of her former companion, and I believed she must have looked on her more as a daughter or a friend.

"Would you please describe Catherine?" I asked as gently as I could.

"You do not know her?" she asked, her tone sharpened, and I saw that anger was an easier emotion for Lady Morcar to express at the moment than sadness was.

"I do not," I said, though I wondered if perhaps I had gotten a glimpse of her on the day we returned the carbuncle; bright red hair and the swish of a woman's skirt rounding a corner.

The countess continued. "Well, she is Scottish, as I said, though she lived in England much of her life. She was raised by her grandmother after her parents died, and was educated by tutors until her grandmother could send her to Switzerland to university. As I said before, Catherine is exceedingly clever, and I was quite pleased when she agreed to become my companion."

"How did that come about, actually?" I asked. The question of red hair still hadn't been answered, but I felt certain this was the woman.

"We met at a gathering at Westfield House. She was newly returned from Switzerland and had come with a friend of my niece. We rapidly moved beyond talk of the weather, thank heavens, into conversations of politics, history, finance, and architecture, and by the end of the evening, I'd asked her if she would consider being my paid companion."

"She sounds quite extraordinary," I said.

"She is. That she stole the carbuncle doesn't change my opinion of her. Would that she had come to me directly rather than resort to dishonesty." There was fierce pride in Lady Morcar's voice, and I thought it would break her heart to hear that Catherine had perhaps engineered considerably more than the simple theft of a gemstone.

"Lady Morcar, does Catherine Cusack have red hair?" I finally asked, nearly holding my breath on the slim chance the answer was no.

Her eyes softened, and her face lit in a warm smile. "The most glorious riot of red curls I've ever seen. How I wished for hair like hers when I was young. It very nearly had a life of its own, and she constantly despaired of keeping it contained in a knot; therefore, she rarely did." Her gaze sharpened to mine again. "If you should see Catherine, Mr. Devereux, I would have you give her this, if you please."

She reached behind her neck and unclasped the chain that held the blue carbuncle, then dropped both chain and jewel into my hand.

I gaped at her. "Lady Morcar, I may never meet Catherine Cusack to give her this."

"You may not, but then you will bring it back to me and tell me the rest of the story."

She stood to indicate our time was up and escorted us to the door.

"Lady Morcar, it has been a true pleasure to meet you," I said, taking her offered had and brushing my lips lightly over the back of it.

She clasped my hand briefly, and I felt the strength of her, and the vulnerability. She turned to Conan Doyle, who had remained raptly silent during our conversation, and offered him her hand as well. Then she opened the door and called to Delilah in her most imperious voice. "See these men to the door, Delilah, and then do not disturb me for an hour."

"Yes, milady," Delilah curtsied respectfully. Yes, this girl was intelligent and had a backbone, but I could see that in her mistress's eyes, she was no Catherine.

Jess met me on the street outside the Langham Hotel. She buzzed with unsaid things, and I needed a moment to think through everything I'd just heard, so I unbuttoned my jacket, looked her in the eye, and said, "First one home gets to speak first."

214

CHAPTER 25 – THE SCANDAL

Tea time at Grayson House was a boisterous affair that afternoon. The weather was lovely – crisp and sunny as it often was just before autumn began in earnest – so we'd left the kitchen door propped open. Reesy, Hannah, and Oliver were in and out with the dogs, popping into the cheery kitchen for bites of treacle tart and sips of tea before running back out to play in the garden.

I caught Charlie's hand in mine across the table and squeezed it. She had the same expression I knew was on my face – one that said *how did this become our life and isn't it wonderful?*

I had finished recounting my version of the afternoon – I was not one to let capable children win races just because they were smaller than I – and now it was Jess's turn.

"Delilah 'as a brain in 'er 'ead, and a good 'eart. She says 'er mistress is generous and kind, once ye get past the snooty tone and manner."

I nodded. That fit with my own impression of Lady Morcar, and I was glad to see that her employee shared my view.

"Delilah came to work for the countess when Miss Cusack went to care for 'er grandmother. Miss Cusack came to visit with Lady Morcar once a week – on Sundays – for those six weeks, and Delilah said she was always very kind to the countess. When Miss Cusack came back to work, Delilah 'ad a couple of days to know 'er, and she admired 'er very much. She thought it right odd then, the night before the carbuncle was returned, to 'ear Miss Cusack in 'er room crying. She knocked to see what she could do for 'er, but the lady pretended nothing was wrong and sent 'er away. But Delilah saw that 'er bag was packed, and Miss Cusack left the next day."

"That was after we'd spoken to Ryder and threatened him with Scotland Yard. He must have gone straight to Catherine and told her the jig was up," I said.

Charlie spoke up. "It doesn't sound as though Miss Cusack wanted to leave her position. Returning to visit the countess every week, despite a leave of absence would seem to indicate that the regard between the women was mutual."

"We know Catherine came to Westfield House with a niece of the countess, so that's a place to begin," I said.

Charlie considered me thoughtfully. "Westfield House is the town house of the current Duke of Westfield. When Queen Victoria visited the place a few years ago, she was said to have told the Duchess, "I've just left my home to come to your palace." The house is considered the finest private home in all of London. One doesn't just accompany someone to Westfield House uninvited." She surprised me with her knowledge of the London social set, as it wasn't something in which we had ever participated.

I exhaled. "All right. So, she's someone with enough of a family name to get herself on a guest list at Westfield House. Perhaps the grandmother, if she exists, is another place to attempt a search?"

"She's got two names that we know of, right?" Jess interjected. "Catherine Cusack and Mrs. MacFarlane. Ye know a Scottish MacFarlane that's a Monger mix, so perhaps MacFarlane is 'er real name and Cusack is an alias?"

"The College of Arms doesn't have Scottish noble records – those are kept at the Court of Lord Lyon in Edinburgh – so we can't look for MacFarlane there."

Jess shook her head. "No, she's not usin' MacFarlane when she's out and about with the posh folk. She used it to let the office and at the bank gettin' the money to buy the necklace at the pawnshop – things she needed proper papers to do. She's usin' Cusack for 'er society life, so that's the name to search at the College of Arms. It may not be *'er* real name, but it's someone's."

I raised my coffee mug to her in a toast. "Well-reasoned, Jess. I'm impressed."

"Cusack is an Irish name," said Charlie. "It's one of the names on the family tree my mother showed me when I was small."

"An Irish Clocker name?" I asked. Charlie's mother had come from a family of time-travelers, and though Charlie herself wasn't skilled as such, she could act as a conduit to amplify the abilities of a Clocker with whom she traveled.

"I don't know. But as a general rule, most of the Irish I've ever met have a bit of *other* blood in them. And if she's a Monger MacFarlane too, she could have quite the variety of skills." Charlie stood and began clearing dishes from the table. Jess jumped up to help her while I put away the leftover stew and vegetables.

The dogs came tearing through the kitchen door and barked their way to the front hall just as the gong could be heard from the doorbell. I caught Charlie's eye. "Expecting someone?"

She shook her head. "It's probably Oscar looking for news of today's adventures." She kissed me quickly. "Go answer it before the dogs frighten him away."

I smirked. "Oscar doesn't frighten easily. You could probably scare him, but our dogs definitely do not." I kissed her back before I left the kitchen, wiping my wet hands on a dishtowel as I went to the door.

I made the dogs sit at attention in the hall before I opened the door — a good thing, as it wasn't Oscar Wilde standing there at all.

A gentleman, richly dressed in a charcoal gray bespoke suit and bright white silk cravat stood on my doorstep. His carriage, bearing the identifiably opulent Westfield arms, was parked on the street, and his driver waited beside the horses. There was an envelope of Barings Bank stationary in his pocket, the contents of which had worried him, according to the worn crease, and he had recently begun drinking rather heavily, if the puffiness of his face and his bloodshot eyes in an otherwise fit countenance could be believed. He also intended to be here awhile, and so I expected I would have to invite the man into my home.

"Your Grace," I said to the Duke of Westfield. "How may I be of service?"

He had the same haughty tone that Lady Morcar used to such great effect, as though it were an unconscious element of their upbringing, and he indicated no surprise that I knew his identity. "You are Devereux?" he said with a slight sneer.

"I am. Would you do me the honor?" I stepped back from the door and gestured for him to enter. Mercifully, the dogs didn't move from their sphinxlike poses.

He sniffed, probably unconsciously, but the effect was to convey disdain. The man was about my size and somewhere in his forties, but his demeanor made it seem as though he thought himself infinitely more venerable and worthy of respect.

I rolled down my shirt sleeves and directed him to the study, which was the most masculine room in the house, primarily

219

because I hadn't changed anything from the previous occupant. Reesy came careening around the corner and stopped short at the sight of the duke's top hat and formal coat. "Go ask Charlie to bring tea to the study," I half-whispered to him. I hoped he would have the sense to mention the appearance of the nobleman in our foyer.

The Duke of Westfield stood by a window overlooking the street, and he didn't turn when I closed the door. "I understand you are looking for my cousin's companion."

"If your cousin is Lady Morcar, then yes, indeed I am."

"I would like to be informed when you locate her," he said, as though that was all he needed to say.

Why? It was the obvious thing to ask, but instead, I said nothing. I knew that people became uncomfortable with a silence that was allowed to stand – and what they said to fill the silence was often most interesting. When my silence had stretched for a full minute, the duke finally turned to face me.

"You will inform me when you find Catherine Cusack?"

Ah, finally a question rather than a command. I leaned back against the desk and crossed my arms in front of my chest. And still I waited. I kept a pleasant expression on my face, and even raised my eyebrows enough to indicate that I expected an explanation. Clearly, the duke was unused to having to provide one, because his discomfort seemed to rise exponentially the longer I didn't speak.

220

Finally, he burst out in frustration. "She has something of mine."

"Then I expect you will have gone to Scotland Yard," I said calmly. There was a tap at the door, and Charlie came in with a tea tray. I had just had coffee and actually had to use the lavatory, but manners dictated that I offer my guest a refreshment. Fortunately, my wife was much more adept at the manners business than I ever would be.

She smiled prettily as she poured him a cup of tea. "How do you do, Your Grace? I am Charlotte Devereux. Do you take milk or sugar with your tea?"

She'd startled him into answering. "Sugar if you please, two." He took the cup she offered and smiled his thanks. It was a nice change from the scowl he'd worn when she walked in. "Thank you, Mrs. Devereux."

"You're welcome." She touched my hand lightly on her way out, her back to the duke. "*Other*," she mouthed, so that only I could see. "Please let me know if you'd like some sandwiches, won't you?" she said, to cover the silent word.

Fascinating. The Duke of Westfield was an *other* of some variety. Until I had a chance to speak privately with Charlie, I would have no idea if he was a hero or a villain, or, like most of us, something in between. In any case, I had to trust that since she'd left me alone with him and hadn't brought the dogs in, she must not think him too dangerous.

221

"Catherine has letters," he said as soon as the door closed behind Charlie.

"Letters you sent her?"

His scowl had returned. "Yes."

My feelings about that were fairly simple. Don't put anything in writing you wouldn't want the world to read when you're dead. So I let my silence, once again, fill the void.

"I'm to be re-married," he said in a tone somewhere between misery and anger. I couldn't tell whether the tone was because of Catherine Cusack or because of his impending marriage. I decided it was prudent not to ask, and was amusing myself with everything I *didn't* say.

"Your Grace, if you were my brother—" he looked appalled at the effrontery, but I smiled benignly and continued. "I would advise you to tell your fiancée that you once harbored an attraction for another woman, but as soon as you met your fiancée, all thoughts of any other woman left you entirely. And then I would suggest you pretend the letters don't exist, and if they ever do come to light, you can smile and say to your wife, 'But darling, I told you about her before we were married. You know she meant nothing to me once I met you.' You are a man. Men are forgiven for indiscretions – God knows why, but we are. Women, on the other hand, are ruined by them, which is why I don't believe the letters will ever surface – Miss Cusack has everything to lose while you have very little, except perhaps a bit of dignity."

The duke's scowl deepened and became something fierce and decidedly ignoble. I wondered if perhaps I had poked the wrong sort of *other* with my unwelcome attempt at brotherly advice.

"A loss of dignity is most unacceptable. I need those letters, Devereux, and either you can get them for me, or I'll send someone else after them – someone who will not care in whose way he gets or how he achieves his aim."

I managed to keep my expression neutral, though my eyes narrowed at him as I spoke. "I do not respond to threats, Your Grace. If, in the course of my search for Catherine Cusack, I happen upon letters you've written to her, I may return them to you. If you send someone after her, she will run. She is a person of interest to Scotland Yard, and if she feels threatened in any way, you can be sure she will lash out. It is in your best interest, therefore, to allow me to find her quickly and quietly, before the Metropolitan Police and their detectives do. To that end, any information you may have on Miss Cusack's possible whereabouts would be very helpful."

He glared at me for a long moment, and I didn't relax my stance. If someone had entered the study just then, they would have seen two seething granite statues of men trying not to swing at each other. Finally, he nodded and held out a card. On it was a handwritten address in Belgravia.

"She keeps a flat there," he snarled.

"And what of your own attempts to reclaim the letters?"

"She has barred the door to me since I—well, it was one time, and she won't see me alone since then."

"You struck her." I was angrier than I'd been since the duke arrived, and the dogs must have sensed it because one of them barked. I went to the study door and opened it. "Good day, Your Grace."

"My letters—"

"I will contact you if I retrieve them." I looked him in the eyes when he passed by me, and he was first to look away. It was a simple dominance maneuver, but I had won and he knew it.

The dogs were still seated where I had left them in the foyer, much to my complete shock, and they watched the duke warily until he had opened the front door and let himself out. The minute he was gone, they bounded over to me and bumped my legs for the attention they deserved for being so well-mannered.

I slid down the door frame to sit on the floor with them. Gryf threw himself across my lap while Huff tried to wiggle under my arm for a belly rub. Charlie found us like that several minutes later.

"He comes from an old line of Etanian druin," she said quietly.

"Druin rather than druid? I've never heard that word."

"Most people haven't. They're very proud, and the males behave like wolves when they feel threatened," she explained.

I laughed without humor. "Well then, I just won a dominance round that won't sit well with him. I suppose I should watch my back now."

Charlie rubbed my shoulder, and I leaned into her hand just like the dogs were doing to me. "It's probably not wise to make an enemy of a duke," I sighed.

She shrugged. "What's the worst that could happen?"

I took her hand and kissed her palm. "My generator could explode and blow up the house."

Charlie's laugh made me happy to my soul. "See, a duke has nothing on the mayhem you could conjure all by yourself."

"That's not comforting," I grumbled.

She sat herself on the floor next to me, arranging the long skirts she wore so they didn't get crushed by dogs. "You have hounds for comfort, and you have me to love you no matter what you do, who you anger, or how you feel."

I leaned my head back against the wall. "Jess and I ran back from the Langham today, and she took a tumble off a rather high brick wall that was a challenging climb for me. She rolled and popped right up, and I was incredibly proud of her. But for the space of a heartbeat, I was frightened she'd been hurt, and half a heartbeat later, angry that I'd been afraid for her. I managed to grit my teeth and say nothing, but for a moment I thought that must

225

be what it's like to be a parent, with pride and fear and anger all jumbled together into a messy bundle of something that makes your stomach hurt and your heart burst."

She traced my fingers with hers. "You make me fall in love with you a little more each day I know you, and I've been all the way in love for a long time."

"Thank you for opening your heart to me, and our home to those irregular misfits we seem to have taken in," I said softly.

"The more there is to love, the more love there is, and those misfits are in need of a bath and a story." She stood and pulled me to my feet, then wrapped her arms around my waist. "I love you," she whispered into my chest.

I held her tightly, and felt our heartbeats pound together as one.

Chapter 26 – Belgravia

Jess had already scouted the Belgravia address of Catherine Cusack by the time I arrived. I was late, having stopped along the way to pay the food accounts for our much-increased household. I was still grumbling about the size of the baker's bill.

Jess snapped something about growing children, and then directed my attention to the fact that it appeared someone was home. We both realized it was probably best to go through the front door rather than try to break in.

"You're going to have to bloody my lip then," I said to Jess, as I stood in a doorway hidden from view of the flat.

She stared at me in surprise. "Why?"

"A woman alone would be foolish to open the door to a man for no reason. A man who's been hurt has a much better chance of being allowed in to be helped."

Jess rolled her eyes at me like I was the biggest idiot she knew. "A man carryin' a child that's been 'urt 'as an even better chance of gettin' into the flat than a man with a bloody lip."

"Indeed," I said dryly. Ten-year-old pickpockets could be annoyingly clever.

She stuck her tongue out at me and then fainted dead away.

I barely caught her in my arms, and very nearly panicked. "Jess?" I said frantically. She cracked an eyelid.

"Shut it and go ring the bell," she murmured.

She was good, I'd give her that … right after I throttled her for scaring me – again.

"I'd be surprised if she keeps anything of value in that flat, otherwise, why allow Westfield to have the address?" I staggered a little as I rang the bell.

"One way to find out," Jess whispered, just as the door opened.

"This child just collapsed in front of your house. Can you help me?" I said in a frantic voice as I pushed myself into the doorway. The young woman who answered the door backed away.

"I'll get my mistress," she said as she ran up the stairs.

I followed her up, and was tempted to hurl Jess over my shoulder like a sack of potatoes. She was heavy. "Don't even think about it," she warned quietly.

"You're a lump," I murmured, shifting her in my arms.

"Get stronger then," she whispered back.

Thankfully, there was a sitting room just at the top of the stairs. I laid Jess out on the sofa and immediately scanned the room for whatever information I could glean.

The place reminded me a bit of my own secret flat above the accountancy office near the river. I had only been there once since Charlie and I had moved into Grayson House, but it was part of my old life as someone whose only responsibility was to himself and the business of staying alive. Here, there were stacks of books on the floor and on every available surface, with papers tucked between their pages. There were drawings pinned to the walls – architectural drawings that reminded me of my days as a thief, when studying the layout of a building was essential to finding its exits. The furniture was old, but of fine quality, and a tattered quilt of heavy plaids lay spread over the back of the sofa.

I had only enough time to flip two books open and look at the papers stuffed inside before the sound of footsteps in the hall alerted me to an approaching woman.

The woman.

My first impression was of the very aptly described riot of red curls, and in that moment I understood the use of hair as a distractionary device. I also had the vague impression that I knew her from somewhere, which was odd, because though I may have seen her hair at the Langham Hotel, I had never seen her face. My second impression was that of my own heart slamming in my chest. I was nervous to meet her, and the thought actually made

229

me smile at my own ridiculousness. My third impression was that she wasn't surprised to see me, though perhaps the smile did throw her a little.

"How is the child?" she said in a low, breathless voice. The voice was an act meant to seduce, and it would have worked very easily had I been remotely vulnerable to seduction. Catherine Cusack, if indeed that was her name, was a few years older than I, of average height, above average beauty, extraordinary hair, and something electric that sizzled just under the surface of every movement and every expression. At the moment, her outward expression was one of concern, but underneath it was something closer to excitement. I felt it too, so I recognized it for what it was.

She knew of me and was intrigued.

I made a show of feeling Jess's forehead as though checking for a temperature. "Waking up, I think."

Her eyes fluttered open, and she ignored me and went straight for the source of the voice. I thought Jess was as eager for a glimpse of the woman as I had been.

"What 'appened?" she said in a groggy tone. Jess was a fair actress, and I would have believed her if I'd been gullible. But no one in the room was, and the woman seemed to come to the same conclusion. She rocked back on her heels and then held out her hand to me.

"Ringo Devereux, I presume? And Jess, your newly adopted pickpocket. It is interesting to finally meet you."

I shook her hand and was surprised to find it so cold. "I am sorry. My disadvantage is that I'm not quite sure what to call you. Catherine Cusack seems to do well for social situations, and Mrs. MacFarlane for legal ones, but as this circumstance is neither, I am at a loss."

She smiled at the parry, but it was still a mask. "MacFarlane is my grandmother's name, and as she raised me, it is my legal name. Cusack is the name I was born with, but you can call me Elizabeth."

"Elizabeth MacFarlane. I don't suppose I'll find any record of a family history with that name?"

This time her smile was genuine. "You can try."

Jess sat up on the sofa and was watching the conversation with avid interest as Elizabeth perched on the edge of a chair and relaxed herself into a pose that looked practiced. It was very attractive on her, so I assumed she had found good use for it in the past, but I was much more interested in the fact that she seemed to think it would work on me.

"Why Westfield?" I asked with far less tact that one generally should when questioning someone's taste in partners.

"A means to an end."

"He wants his letters back."

She smiled again, the way a feral cat smiles at the rat it intends to disembowel. "He can't have them."

I shrugged. "Makes no difference to me, except that if I don't give the letters to him, he has promised to send far less interesting goons than I to harass you."

She sighed dramatically. "Ah, but he can be tiresome, can't he? The woman he's about to marry is perfectly dreadful and will take his family for all the money she possibly can when he dies. Really, I should let her have him without a fuss, but an intact fortune is so much easier to steal than one that's tied up in legal proceedings."

"So, mere theft then? That hardly seems sporting when you're clearly so much better armed than he is, and it doesn't really explain the document theft at Barings." I studied her carefully for the slightest twitch to give away her true objective, but she was very, very good.

"Doesn't it? Ah, well, you're not looking at the big picture. And here I thought you were at least as well-armed as I. Poor Ringo, the guilt money left to you by a noble half-brother just doesn't seem to fit your circumstances, especially as the older brother still lives and has no idea who you are. I'm sure a well-placed word in the right ears might make for a very interesting visit from a herald at the College of Arms."

As well-informed as Elizabeth MacFarlane was, she didn't know everything – like, for example, that Archer was not actually related to me by blood, and there was definitely no guilt involved in the bestowing of his name.

She turned to Jess and said sweetly, "go find Mathilda and ask her for some biscuits for yourself, darling. I'm sure he hasn't thought to get you lunch yet today."

Jess met my eyes very briefly before she cast them down and left the room. Once she'd gone, Elizabeth's voice lost its sweetness. "Stay out of my way, Mr. *Devereux*. You will not enjoy the cost of thwarting me." Her emphasis on my name made it very clear what that cost would be, and I disliked how deep the pit of my stomach felt at her words.

I stood and reached into my trouser pocket, and Elizabeth flinched. As angry as she'd just made me, I didn't care for the fact that she reacted like a beaten dog. "I have a message from Lady Morcar," I said, as I held out the carbuncle. "She asked me to give this to you, and she wishes you had gone to her directly. She would have given you whatever you needed."

I'd struck a nerve, and Elizabeth reached a tentative hand out to touch the gemstone. She almost didn't take it, and I could see pride and avarice at war on her face. But then she plucked it from my hand and slipped it into her own pocket.

"I heard it rattling around in her teapot, you know. An ingenious way to return it," her voice was very quiet, as though she spoke to herself rather than to me.

"Why did you stay at the hotel after Ryder told you we'd found the carbuncle?"

Elizabeth scoffed in a very unladylike manner. "Ryder was a foolish man who sought my favor. I actually hoped to intercept whoever would be returning the stone."

I scowled. "To steal it again?"

She met my scowl with one of her own. "To bring it to the countess myself, and thereby remove any need to leave her service."

Suddenly, the maid burst into the sitting room, and the smell of smoke came with her, filling the space. "Mistress! There's a fire in the kitchen!"

I knew better than to look at the maid. Instead, I watched Elizabeth, and I saw her eyes dart at the mantle of the fireplace, to the left pillar, and with that look, I knew where she'd hidden the letters.

Just then, someone pounded on the front door below us, and Elizabeth and I stared at each other. She moved swiftly to the window, and I joined her there to see two men with the build of dockworkers getting ready to kick the door in. "Westfield's men," I said. In my anger at the duke, I had not convinced him that I would get the letters, so he had taken matters into his own hands. I turned to Elizabeth and was startled to find her face so close to mine. "Run!"

I wasn't sure why I wanted her to escape them, except that they would likely hurt her. And besides being somewhat innately chivalrous in my instinct to protect women, I found that my curiosity about her was an oddly provocative motivation to see her safe to match wits with another day.

"I need—" She was suddenly frantic, and her eyes leapt to the fireplace mantle again.

"Just go!" They were pounding up the stairs now, and I rushed to the side of the entry. Elizabeth grabbed Mathilda, and they raced toward the back of the flat just as two East End thugs slammed into the room carrying clubs.

The first one rushed in without spotting me, and I tripped the second one so he went down hard, falling forward and tangling with thug number one on his way down.

The first thug wrestled his way free and swung at me. I dodged behind the sofa and was rewarded with the crack of wood where the club hit the frame. The other man was struggling to his feet, but his club had rolled in my direction. I grabbed it before he could, and swung.

My blow was hard enough to crack bone, and certainly hard enough to make a man howl. Thug two went down again, holding his knees, and thug one faced me across the room.

"Ye don't want to do this, mate," he growled at me. He wasn't wrong. I really didn't want to do this. But even less did I want to leave these two to their own devices in this flat. I didn't know whether Jess and the women had escaped, or even if the fire Jess must have set in the kitchen was still burning, but my first priority, after dodging thug one's club, was to get to whatever Elizabeth had hidden in her fireplace.

He lunged at me, which was predictable given that he was twice my size and weight. He hadn't expected my agility though, and I launched myself off the sofa and over him, dropping the club I still held on his head as I leapt. It was a spectacular move, even if I did say so myself.

The contact was enough to knock him down, and even better, he dropped his own club. I lunged for him, but Elizabeth, appearing as if from the ether, got there first, his club in her hand, and she struck. His head sounded remarkably like the wooden frame of the sofa had done, and I winced at the thud his body made when it hit the floor. Thug two cried out and curled into a tight ball, protecting his head as if he knew he was next.

Elizabeth looked at me, almost as if ascertaining whether I'd been hurt. A club remained in each of our hands. I thought it likely that she was prepared to use hers, but I was next to the fireplace, so I took a risk.

Still facing her, with my club in one hand, I reached the other behind me and felt along the woodwork.

"What are you doing?" she asked me, though she knew the answer already.

"Relieving you of your letters so more of them—" I indicated the two men on the floor, "don't come for you."

She scoffed. "So it's an altruistic motive then, is it?" She took a step toward me, and the club in her hand raised an inch or two.

"Something like that," I said, just as my fingers found the catch. I pressed it, and a piece of the wood trim popped open behind my head.

"Don't do this, Devereux," she said in a voice that sounded almost like a plea wrapped in a snarl.

Thug two tried to crawl toward the door, and I used the momentary distraction to remove a stack of documents from the cubby and stuff it into my pocket.

Elizabeth screamed in frustration, and she swung the club at thug two, who just barely darted out of the door and ran away down the stairs. Then she stalked toward me, the club raised like a fist. "Give me the letters, Ringo!" It was definitely a snarl this time, and I had to tap her club out of the way as if it were a sword.

She swung again and connected with my club hard enough to jar my arm. "I will hurt you, and I will hate myself for a minute because you're a worthy adversary. But then I'll get over it, and you'll still be injured ... or worse. I don't want to do that, Ringo. Give me the letters!"

I edged back again, and Elizabeth stalked toward me, the rage writ loud on her face. "The letters!"

237

I took the packet of baker's receipts from my trouser pocket and flung them into the fireplace. Elizabeth screamed and dove after them as I darted down the hall and into the kitchen where Jess stood with the rear window wide open and a piece of burnt toast in one hand.

"Took ye long enough," she said calmly as she leapt out of the window, onto the rear balcony, and down the ladder to escape into the back alley. I was right on her heels and just barely caught the sound of Elizabeth's furious voice as she screamed, "RINGO!!!"

Chapter 27 – Among Friends

The Langham Hotel was quite peaceful in the hours between lunch and dinner on a weekday afternoon. Arthur Conan Doyle and Oscar Wilde sat across from me, listening raptly to the tale of my narrow escape from a club-wielding, Medusa-haired, master criminal who had engineered not one, but three adventures for me to stumble upon in the space of a single month.

I had waited a day to send Scotland Yard to the Belgravia flat, hopeful that Elizabeth hadn't actually killed the thug she'd clubbed. They'd found blood on the floor, but otherwise the flat was empty and clean. It had been rented under the name Catherine Cusack, who seemed to have fled in the night with all her belongings, and I silently wished her a safe journey in hopes she'd actually left London. It wasn't likely, but given that I'd allowed her to escape rather than brave her temper, her club, and my own conflicted conscience, it was far better than the alternative.

I'd admitted to Charlie that I'd read the letters before returning them to the Duke of Westfield. There were no state secrets contained within, and nothing particularly incriminating beyond his disdain for his family and the fact that he seemed to have already been engaged while he carried on a love affair with Catherine.

I called her Catherine in relation to Westfield, because that's what he called her in his letters. It also separated her from the very clever, quite fascinating woman I'd met who was worth ten Dukes of Westfield.

Charlie had been as intrigued by Elizabeth MacFarlane as I, and we'd spent hours the night before discussing the things Jess and I had learned about her. She was well-educated, as Lady Morcar had said, and as the books on finance, banking, money-lending, history, and economics in her flat had confirmed. The paper I'd seen in a finance tome was a copy of the Westfield family tree, and I recognized the College of Arms seal on the top, so perhaps her threat to steal the duke's entire fortune hadn't been an idle one. It was also quite interesting that Lady Morcar was Westfield's cousin, and that Elizabeth had been employed with her as Catherine for the previous six months. Elizabeth was clearly a skilled and patient plotter, and her attention to detail was as disconcerting as it was impressive. Her theft of the carbuncle was the only thing that felt more like an impulsive crime of opportunity than part of what I was beginning to suspect was a much larger plot. I was quite certain that London had not seen the last of Elizabeth MacFarlane.

Westfield's arrogance still rankled though, and part of me was sorry that Elizabeth's plan to expose him to his fiancée had failed. Charlie reminded me that Elizabeth had already had a bit of revenge on him when she very nearly collapsed Barings Bank, of which he was a major shareholder. Oddly, it made me feel better.

It was Jess's discovery, however, that was the most promising lead on Elizabeth's true identity. Jess had slipped into the bedroom at the Belgravia flat while the maid tried to put out the fire. The room was empty of any personal items at all except for one drawing pinned to the back of the door, visible to the bed where only Elizabeth could see it. The drawing was a study of a sleeping woman's face, a close-up in pencil and chalk that I recognized as a detail of Frederic Leighton's *Flaming June*. It was the face of Elizabeth MacFarlane.

Having the appropriate amount of scruples for the circumstances, Jess had rolled the paper up and stuck it in her coat. The drawing was now pinned to the wall in the library where Charlie's faun painting had once hung, and Charlie was so enamored with the artistry of the drawing that I thought she might have it framed.

At the Langham Hotel, I sat with men who had become my friends. The taciturn Scot was perhaps an odder choice of friend than the flamboyant poet was, but I enjoyed the intelligence and wit that infused every conversation with them, and I had begun to look forward to our encounters.

"You realize you've made a very clever enemy, don't you?" said Conan Doyle seriously.

"It would almost be entertaining," I replied, "except that she's quite possibly much cleverer than I, and certainly more ruthless. I don't look forward to seeing her locked up, though I admit, I'll likely sleep better at night when she is."

"What else do you know about her identity?" Oscar asked.

"I have a lead to follow in London when a certain artist returns from France." I eyed Oscar meaningfully before continuing. "Otherwise, I'm not quite certain how to check on the Scottish family connections," *in this time*, I almost added. A quick computer search in a twenty-first-century library would likely take care of all my information needs.

"The Lyon Court in Edinburgh is the only way," said Conan Doyle.

"If you do make a journey to Scotland, consider a visit to Cragside in Northumberland. I hear Armstrong has dammed his river and is using hydroelectric power to light his house," said Oscar with a wink.

Damn him. He knew precisely which sparks would ignite my imagination. My smile was closer to a grimace. "And you'll come with me if I go?"

"Good Lord, no! I'm Irish. We know better than to get within a hundred miles of Scotland. Those Scots are fearsome." He gave a mock shudder, and Conan Doyle snickered.

I stood to go. "I'm off to instruct some feral children how to read. Charlie has begun teaching small classes of children at the Workhouse, so I am in charge of our own irregular misfits' education."

Oscar chuckled at that, and I thought I would do well to rope him into helping me.

"Did you tell Lady Morcar about your encounter with her companion?" Conan Doyle asked as he shook my hand.

"I told the countess that I'd given Catherine the carbuncle, and that she'd been moved to silence. The countess laughed at that and said that Catherine must have been very moved indeed if she hadn't a clever or cutting response. She seemed quite touched by Catherine's reaction though, as I believe she genuinely cared for her." I had not mentioned the affair with Westfield to the countess, as I felt it didn't reflect the best of a very bright woman.

"Until next time, gentlemen." I departed the Langham with a smile and a tip of the hat from John Hartwell, the doorman, as I walked out of the building.

The weather was properly crisp now, and the fashionable jacket and cravat Charlie had made me wear were far less uncomfortable than they'd been merely a month ago. Nonetheless, I looked forward to getting back to Grayson House and changing into my beloved jeans before sitting on the floor with dogs and irregular misfits to read them all stories.

"Ye've got a suspicious smile on yer face. It's like ye know a secret," Jess said, falling into step beside me.

"I do," I said, suddenly sure of the next step. "I know the last one home is going to Scotland with me."

The End

THE REAL HISTORY

I became acquainted with Oscar Wilde when I was
researching book five of the Immortal Descendants series, and
when I discovered that Oscar Wilde, Arthur Conan Doyle, and the
editor of Lippincott's magazine had dined together on August 30,

1889 at the Langham Hotel, I knew what the future had in store for Ringo.

I've always loved the Sherlock Holmes mysteries, and I've delighted in all the ways storytellers have played with the canon of Conan Doyle's timeless tales. My favorite is the BBC's recent *Sherlock*, for its modern take on the stories, and I hope the surly Scot who wrote them might have understood that fan fiction of the breadth, depth, and variety Sherlock Holmes has enjoyed is a compliment of the highest order.

For those who may not recognize the mysteries in which Ringo engaged, first was *The Adventure of the Blue Carbuncle*, followed by *The Red-Headed League*, and then finally, a rendition of *A Scandal in Bohemia*.

As in the Immortal Descendants series – the time travel fantasies in which the character of Ringo is introduced – considerable truth is woven throughout the fiction. The National Library of Scotland hosts a map overlay on their site that is an invaluable research tool. One can see the modern map of London beneath an overlay of the survey maps that go back as far as 1885. Many of the buildings and locations I wrote about, including the St. Marylebone Workhouse, The Ossington Estates, the Grosvenor Gallery, and the Ragged Schools, can be found on those maps. Here is the link text to the website for anyone interested in seeing what the Victorian city of London actually looked like: http://maps.nls.uk/geo/explore/#.

Barings Bank, with its overextended Argentine loans, was at the center of the Panic of 1890, a financial crisis which could have resulted in the collapse of the British economy. The Bank of England and N.M. Rothschild & Sons, among others, had to prop up Barings in order to keep the institution from failing completely. Barings was, in fact, the legal entity that sold the Louisiana Territory to the United States, though it did so for Napoleon with the blessing of British politicians, despite the fact that the money essentially funded the French war effort against the English.

The surviving wine cellar of Whitehall has a fascinating history, as it was actually encased in concrete and moved slightly to accommodate the building of the British Ministry of Defense. An excellent blog at www.ediblegeography.com/the-last-places/ includes current pictures of the cellar as well as historical ones, and features a map of all the buildings in the original Whitehall Palace complex. Apparently, part of the tennis court and cock-fighting pit have also been incorporated into government buildings in the modern Whitehall complex.

There truly is a Victorian operating theater tucked into the tower of St. Thomas Church in Southwark, which lay forgotten and undiscovered until 1956. The plague pits under St. Bride's Church weren't discovered until a World War II bombing raid exposed areas below the crypt. Archeologists found bodies from the plague of 1666 as well as from a cholera epidemic in 1854 buried there.

Leighton House is a museum to the art and life of Frederic Leighton. It contains the extraordinary Arab Hall, as well has many of his paintings. *Flaming June*, one of his most recognizable artworks, was lost for thirty years before being discovered behind a false wall, hanging over a fireplace in a private home. It now has its permanent home at the Museo de Arte de Ponce in Puerto Rico, and was not damaged during the recent hurricane. The Grosvenor Gallery was considered the seat of Aesthetic exhibitions in London from 1877 until it closed in 1890, and Oscar Wilde wrote reviews for two of its shows. The power substation behind the Grosvenor Gallery was responsible for lighting several neighborhoods around it with coal and steam-powered generators, and even after the gallery closed, it remained a power-generating substation for many years.

My favorite bits of true history in *An Urchin of Means* are the technological ones. London's gas streetlights were in the process of being replaced in 1890, though there are still 1500 gaslamps throughout modern London, which are lit each night by five lamplighters. Cragside, in Northumberland, was remarkable for having been the first private home in the world to be lit by electricity derived from water power. Its owner, Lord Armstrong, was an arms manufacturer and an amateur engineer. He dammed the river on his property to create five lakes and a hydroelectric power plant. The house itself was a marvel of modern technology, and included a water-powered laundry, sawmill, an electric dishwasher, dumbwaiter, rotisserie, and vacuum cleaner – all lit by Joseph Swan's incandescent lamps. The Wikipedia entry for Cragside is fantastic, and has much more information than the official National Trust site does: https://en.wikipedia.org/wiki/Cragside.

The facts Ringo states about lascar sailors, pawnshops, carbuncles, the Tyburn River, Marylebone, and the College of Arms, are all true. As I am an author of historical fiction who regularly falls down rabbit holes of unexpected research into tantalizingly obscure bits of information, it is utterly delightful to have a character who can follow me down and make such interesting use of it all.

Thank you for joining Ringo and Jess on their Sherlockian adventures in Victorian London. If you'd like to follow news about the next books in the series, receive sneak peeks of chapters, and get early access to exclusive stories, please sign up for my once-a-month newsletter at aprilwhitebooks.com. You can also find sign-up information there for my private reader group, and ways to find me on social media. I love to connect with readers, and I deeply appreciate the support and kindness I've received from the people who stumble over my books and take a moment to share and review them.

If you've never read the Immortal Descendants series, and would like to meet Ringo and Charlie as Saira did, you can find information and links to all five books at aprilwhitebooks.com or at your favorite e-retailer. Thank you so much for being readers. As Ringo might say, **"You can tell a reader by the imagination and possibility with which they view the world."**

Made in the USA
San Bernardino, CA
12 January 2018